Historical Novel Society North America
Last Vegas Short Story Collection

Desert
of
Dreams

Lisa Ard * Sally Bays * Ana Brazil

Julianne Douglas * B. K. Froman

Deborah Grochau * Kurt Larsen

Laura Mace * Leah Moyes * Sally Milliken

Linda Saether * Suzanne Uttaro Samuels

Historical Novel Society North America
hnsna@hns-conference
www.hns-conference.com

ISBN: 979-8-9989693-1-7

Cover Design: Jenny Quinlan

Project Manager: Mary K. Tilghman
Copy editors: Carol M. Cram, Jenny Quinlan, Mary K. Tilghman

Printed and bound in the United States of America

All proceeds from sales of this book are going directly to the nonprofit Historical Novel Society North America (www.hns-conference.com) to assist them with programming of benefit to historical novelists.

Contents

Introduction

LAS VEGAS IS A LAND where dreams come true—and sometimes where they go to die. Neon-spangled some days, rough-hewn on others, the city's history isn't long, but it's colorful.

In 2025, the board of the Historical Novel Society North America chose to hold its conference at Caesars Palace in Las Vegas. It's a great place to bring together historical novelists—from award-winning longtime authors to writers seeking to publish their first book—to discuss their craft and learn from each other.

With Las Vegas set as the conference venue for 2025, the board decided to fill HNSNA's first short story anthology with tales set in this city of casinos, mobsters, neon, and arid desert.

HNSNA has held its biennial conference since 2005. Guests of honor have included Bernard Cornwell, Diana Gabaldon, Margaret George, and Geraldine Brooks. This year, HNS2025 is thrilled to welcome Silvia Moreno-Garcia, Fiona Davis, Sarah Penner, Jeffrey Blount, and Yangsze Choo.

Beginning in 2021, the HNSNA conference has enabled virtual attendance—and drawn participants from around the globe.

The anthology was created to celebrate the HNSNA conference, writers of historical fiction, and the conference location. Authors from around the world were invited to submit a story of up to four thousand words set in or around Las Vegas fifty or more years ago. Over seventy-five authors entered stories. This year's anthology contains the twelve winning stories that celebrate the many faces of Las Vegas, from wistful to cynical.

Stories are presented in chronological order, from its cowboy beginnings through the Atomic Age to the nights when Elvis was king.

Suzanne Uttaro Samuels and Sally Milliken remember when Las Vegas was little more than a dusty patch of desert. In "Doorway to the Desert," Samuels recounts how Helen Stewart, later considered the "First Lady of Las Vegas," chose to stay on her land after her husband's murder. Milliken brings to life the story of Stewart's sons, who can't forget their father's murder, in "Cowboy Justice."

"One of Our Own" by Leah Moyes conjures up 1920s Vegas, when neon was bright and new and cruel men lurking in dark corners could be dangerous.

Laura Mace's haunting "Lady Luck" transports readers to the construction of the Hoover Dam, as seen through the eyes of a skilled and fearless Native American laborer.

A greasy spoon is the setting of Sally Bays's "A Hot Vegas," where a mobster's girl takes refuge in the arms of the guy behind the counter.

In her dual timeline tale "The Last Frontier," Deborah Grochau recalls when singer Josephine Baker faced down racism in a 1952 nightclub—a moment that changed another woman's life.

In the 1950s, atom bomb tests were both a serious Cold War reality and a source of late-night entertainment. B.K. Froman recounts the determination of a Civil Defense official in the face of mounting opposition to the tests in "Up and Atom." Julianne Douglas takes readers inside a bar for a front-seat look at a mushroom cloud—with a cocktail and maybe a spy—in "A Flash in the Pan."

In "Millie & Loretta at the Desert Oasis," Ana Brazil tells the story of a disillusioned wife who meets a sympathetic woman to help her find freedom.

The night the Beatles performed in Las Vegas is recalled in a darkly humorous noir story, "A Hard-Boiled Day's Night," by Kurt Larsen, about a cynical journalist and a dame who may or may not be called Nancy, whom somebody wants to kill. Larsen's story was named the grand-prize winner in the HNSNA anthology contest.

And what would Vegas be without Elvis? Lisa Ard's "Fools Fall in Love" recounts the story of a young fan aiming to stop his wedding to Priscilla in 1967. In "Twenty Minutes to Showtime," Linda Saether takes readers backstage with Elvis near the end of his Las Vegas reign.

We'd like to thank the talented authors who submitted their stories. Thanks, also, to the team of conscientious reviewers who read every submission and to our celebrity judges, Fiona Davis, Eliza Knight, and Heather Webb, who selected the grand prize-winning entry.

Doorway to the Desert

Suzanne Uttaro Samuels

Los Vegas Rancho, 1884

IN MY HANDS, I HELD THE SCRAWLED NOTE:

Mrs. Stewart send a Team and take Mr. Stewart away he is dead. Signed Conrad Kiel

The babe inside stirred as if he knew: Our lives would never be the same. Clutching the paper, I rushed to the corral. My horse, Dolly, was still saddled after the morning ride to the Paiute village to bring willow for another basket. Nipe called to me that she and Santiago, the ranch foreman, would bring the buckboard. Nipe, with eyes seeing things as they were and would be.

The Kiel place was just over a mile north. I rode at full speed, dirt and stones clattering under Dolly's hooves. I didn't think about how the jostling may have hurt the babe; I focused only on the effort of staying upright.

Anyway, I'd birthed four children in eight years. All delivered in the wilds of Nevada, far from the mahogany birthing chair and toile-covered bedchambers of my parents' Sacramento home. I'd been afraid, but Archibald said it would be all right. It had been: two boys and two girls. Healthy and strong. Now this one. Born into a world where his father was dead.

But that couldn't be. Archibald could arm wrestle a man half his age. He could keep pace with even the fastest cowboys on the range. Out here in the desert, people were always imagining things. A green flash at dawn, the shimmer of heat

5

dancing on our rooftop in late afternoon. And water. Always water. Whatever Kiel thought he'd seen, he had to be mistaken. I don't remember getting off my horse when I got to his ranch. All at once, I was running toward the house.

"Where is he? Where is my husband?" I was screaming, but my voice sounded far away.

The front door swung open. Conrad Kiel stepped out, along with his foreman, Parrish. Behind them was Schuyler Henry, the troublemaker Archibald had gone there to fire. The three sauntered over to a blanket-covered heap on the ground. Parrish pulled off the blanket. There was my beloved, a bullet hole through his right temple. Perfectly round, although the skin around it was singed and lacerated.

When I plucked the buckshot from my eldest boy's leg after a shooting mishap last year, it left holes like these. He'd been on his feet by the next day.

I took Archibald's hand and looked into his eyes, searching for a spark. A glimmer.

There was nothing.

The buckboard pulled up behind me. Santiago jumped down. When he greeted Kiel and the others, his voice was deferential. The men waved him away, like he was a fly or a buffalo gnat. I felt a surge of anger but reminded myself: We were on Kiel's land. If he or the others wanted us dead—a pregnant woman, a Mexican, and a Paiute—nothing would stop them.

We loaded Archibald onto the wagon. Santiago tied Dolly to the back of the rig.

Henry flashed me a cold smile. He'd started all this, with his poisonous words.

"We should go," Santiago said quietly.

"Yeah, you better git," Kiel said. "In this heat, he won't keep."

Parrish laughed. "He's gonna start to stink. But that won't be a change for the likes of him."

The other ranchers were jealous because Archibald succeeded in everything he did. When old man Goss had our place, the wheat fields were dried up and the soil cracked and parched. When Archibald took it over, he asked the Paiutes for help in building irrigation ditches, then replanted the fields and brought in cattle. That was last year. Los Vegas Rancho was now one of the biggest and wealthiest in Clark County.

Nipe placed her hand on my arm. "Come, Missus Stewart," she whispered, urging me toward the buckboard. Santiago walked close behind. I could see the gleam of his revolver at his waist.

It was a long ride back to the ranch. When we arrived, our cowboys and ranch hands were waiting. They stood solemnly, their hats in their hands and their brown faces downcast. A few helped Santiago with Archibald's body, carefully lifting it from the wagon. Other men might take advantage of the Mexicans. Not Archibald. He paid them fairly and sent for the doctor if they were hurt or sick. They repaid him with their loyalty.

The ranch hands carried Archibald into the kitchen. Nipe and I followed. As we passed the mesquite tree, Nipe snapped off some of its branches. She laid them in the hearth and lit the feathery leaves. An intense, smoky smell filled the room. Archibald's body had been outside most of the day; the mesquite would help mask the odor.

The men laid Archibald on the pine table, next to my littlest one's high chair. I was grateful when one of them took it away.

"Where are the children?" I asked Nipe.

"In the village," she said simply.

A wave of gratitude washed over me. When we moved out here last year from the town of Pony Springs, I was worried I'd feel isolated, so far from the other settlements. But there were Nipe and Cook and the other Paiute women. They'd been my friends, showing me how to coax sunflowers and corn and squash from the arid soil. We'd sat together in their village, our children playing together as I watched them weave their beautiful baskets. I felt a heaviness in my chest.

With Archibald gone, I'd have to leave, too. Women didn't run ranches like Los Vegas. I reminded myself: This was never going to be a permanent home. Once the ranch was established, we would return to Pony Springs or some other town. I'd insisted on it. I hadn't known how fond I'd be of this place.

Nipe brought a bowl of water and some soft linen. I washed the place on Archibald's face where the gunpowder had burned off his whiskers and the terrible wound on his forehead with the caked-on reddish-purple blood. When I was done—and it took so long to wash off that blood—I unbuttoned his tattered shirt. How many times had I repaired a torn cuff or replaced a lost button? I loosened his belt buckle and eased off that wrecked shirt.

I shuddered when I saw the second wound, just above his collarbone. So many nights, I'd lain my cheek against that soft skin. I'd been a girl when we'd married. Archibald had been so tender, introducing me to the ways of married couples.

Then the words came to me: the slanderous accusations Schyler Henry had hurled at me in this kitchen yesterday morning. I was a Jezebel, whoring around the ranch with the Mexicans while Archibald was away doing business. When I told Archibald, he stormed out, vowing to avenge my honor.

Now he was dead.

The sun was low in the sky when I finished washing my dear husband's body and Santiago and Nipe helped me wrap him in the blanket from our bed. When we were done, Santiago stood sheepishly before me, studying the ground.

Again, Nipe placed her cool hand on mine.

"There is no wood for a coffin," she said. "And no time to send from Pony Springs."

The words didn't register. My husband lay there, his body already growing stiff. How could there be no coffin?

"I won't just put him in the ground," I said. There were jackals and vultures and, most terrible of all, carrion beetles. Shiny and black, with clubbed antennae. They'd swarm under and into my Archibald's body before we finished shoveling the dirt on top of him.

I looked around the room. No one would look at me. That's when I saw it: the door leading from the kitchen to the garden.

"We'll use the doors," I said.

Santiago shook his head. "But the coyotes? The wolves?"

Unspoken was that the land was wild. Every week there was another settler lost.

"We need a coffin," I said.

One of the hands offered to stand guard. Another said he would, too.

I thanked them. The truth was I didn't need to worry about the doors. Soon, we'd be gone and the new owners would have to replace them.

But as the hands began removing the hinges, I couldn't help but think about how many times I'd opened that door to friends. Or how my children had run back and forth through that door, laughing and playing chase. Or that first time I'd arrived here, and Archibald had carried me over the threshold like I was a new bride. That door had served us well. Maybe now it would provide shelter and comfort to my dear Archibald.

***

The next morning, I awoke before first light. On my way downstairs, I paused at the threshold of the nursery. The children's beds were still neatly made; the silence, overpowering. A ranch hand was standing sentry in the kitchen, a shotgun slung over his shoulder. Out here, an open door was an open invitation. An armed guard sent a different message.

Nipe handed me a cup of coffee, then ladled out a bowl of oatmeal. She placed this, along with a spoon, on the pine table. I didn't feel like eating. But it would be a long day, with all those two-faced ranchers coming to give their condolences. I needed to keep my strength up, if not for me, for my children. I picked up the spoon.

As I sat there, a trickle of sweat slipped down my back. I had wanted to wait for the coroner to come before we buried Archibald. His report would help convict Henry, Parrish, and Kiel. But it was summer in the Mojave Desert. Archibald's body wouldn't keep. I forced myself to swallow down a few spoonfuls of oatmeal. Then I went into the parlor.

The coffin was perched on two chairs. Santiago must have worked all night. On top were the rosary beads that had belonged to Archibald's mother. I'd never known him to be religious, but he kept that rosary in the small mahogany box where he stored our marriage and birth certificates. Maybe he thought it was good luck. A talisman, like a rabbit's foot or a four-leaf clover.

I was standing next to the coffin, the morning light glinting off the warm oak, when the Paiute women arrived. Pamahas, the tribal elder, came in first. She had deeply etched lines around her mouth and on her forehead. My eldest, William, followed behind. He'd turned ten that spring and had his father's deep-set eyes. Hiram, my eight-year-old, came in next. He was holding the hand of Pamahas's daughter, Winona. His lower lip was quivering. I wanted to go to him and hold him in my arms. But Archibald was always talking about the need for fortitude and self-reliance. Out of respect for my husband, I stayed where I was. The girls came in with Nipe: four-year-old Tiza and the baby, Evaline, each clutching a small corn husk doll.

Before we walked up to the graveyard, Santiago handed me the Bible that Mother had given me when Archibald and I left Sacramento as a newly married couple. I don't think I'd opened it since. Maybe Archibald would have preferred to be buried as a Paiute—his body tucked into one of the limestone cliffs, a clutch of poppies at his feet. We'd never talked about it. I followed the buckboard to a freshly dug hole on the hill. My fingers found those familiar pages in the book of John and I recited the words about the Lord being the resurrection and the life as Archibald was lowered into the ground. My little girls were crying; Hiram, too. But William stood there emotionless beside that old Paiute woman. My chest swelled with pride.

When we returned to the house, Nipe and I laid a spread on the table where Archibald's body had been. A platter of sliced apples and buckwheat bread. A jar of honey. Grapes. All of it taken from the stores intended for my children and the people who worked the farm. The ranchers and their wives arrived soon after to pay their condolences. There must have been twenty of them: men dressed in dove-gray frock coats and silk vests; ladies in fine satin dresses with rustling petticoats. I hated them for the casual way they pointed to the wheat fields in the distance and talked about the price of beef, all the while casting side glances at the spring that still flowed despite the lack of rainfall. I wouldn't miss them when we were gone, but I hated the idea of any of them taking up residence here.

When the platters had been scraped clean and the wine bottles were empty, the ranchers and their wives took their leave of us. From the barn, I could hear my children's laughter as our cowboys showed off their latest rodeo tricks. I lit a lamp and went up to my bedroom. I took out a piece of stationery and a fountain pen and wrote to Father.

I need help, I wrote.

I hated doing it. Maybe because I was the oldest daughter. A stand-in for the son my father never had. Or maybe it felt like a surrender, and I hated losing. But even if I wanted to stay, women didn't manage ranches like Los Vegas on their own. Sure, I could welcome travelers passing through and prepare their meals. That earned a tidy sum. I could farm—and I had, with the help of my Paiute neighbors, coaxing vegetables and fruit from the land. Most of our money, though, came from the Archibald's ranching and hauling businesses. That was men's work. It was hard to imagine the ranchers who'd come here today would ever accept me in his stead.

No. My days in the desert were over. Father would make his way here. He'd engage an agent and sell the ranch. We'd return to California. The children would enroll in school. With the money from the ranch, they'd have every opportunity. The boys would have careers; the girls would marry well. As for me, I'd return to the Sacramento Social Club, although after my years in Nevada, it was hard to imagine sitting through all those lectures and high teas. Just thinking of it made me feel irritable.

Father arrived on the stagecoach eight days later. A layer of fine red dust had settled in his wrinkles, deepening them and making him appear old.

He took me by the arm. "We need to talk." Once inside the parlor, he drew the curtains. "I stopped in Carson City on my way out. I had an appointment with Archibald's lawyer." His lips were pressed tightly together.

I knew what he was going to say before he uttered a word. "There's no will," I said.

"You don't seem surprised."

How many times had I encouraged Archibald to make a will? He kept promising he'd do it. But Carson City was a full day's ride. And he was always so busy.

Father shook his head. "It's hard to believe. Archibald is— or was—such a careful man."

But careful men didn't get themselves shot avenging their wives' honor.

"I'm his wife. Mother to his children. Why should it matter if there's a will?"

Father took my hands. "It'll be all right, dear."

I pulled free. "What do you mean by that?" My voice sounded high. Tight.

"Without a will, Archibald's estate will go to probate. The judge will decide."

"Decide what? This was our ranch. Mine and Archibald's."

"Calm down, Helen," Father said, glancing at my belly. "It isn't good for you to get so emotional."

"What isn't good," I hissed, "is for this baby to be born into poverty, with no father to take care of him."

"No judge would allow that, Helen…"

"This isn't Sacramento, Father. Out here, the law is fickle. Just ask the Mexicans or the Paiutes. Or my Archibald, lying in his grave while the men who killed him still walk free."

The seconds ticked past on the grandfather clock. I started to feel bad for yelling at my father. He'd come all the way out here to help me.

"I'm sorry, Father," I said finally. "Everything we had is sunk into this ranch. Without it, we'll have nothing." I looked Father in the eye. "What do I have to do?"

He blinked hard, seeming to brace himself. "You have to stay on the ranch. Until things are settled."

"But I'm going back with you to Sacramento. I need to get the children settled." No need to tell him that Hiram cried himself to sleep every night or that little Tiza had begun wetting the bed.

"If you leave now, you could lose everything." Father's voice was monotone. "It'll go to auction. Anyone could buy it. For any price."

"But it's worth tens of thousands of dollars…" My voice trailed off. I'd seen the way those ranchers had looked at our wheat. Our heads of cattle. Our burbling spring. The babe inside moved. I think he was thinking as I was: We owed it to Archibald to get a fair price. I asked Father how long we'd have to stay.

"A year," Father answered. "Maybe two. Just until the judge in Carson City decides. Once it's yours, you can sell it. Free and clear."

On the ranch, I was as good as any ranch hand or cowboy. I could stay in the saddle for hours. Rope a calf in record time. Help bring in a herd of cattle. But out in the world, I had no more rights than a child.

"They'll let me inherit it?" I asked. "Even though I'm a woman?"

13

Father nodded. "They've just changed the law. When a man dies without a will, half his estate goes to his wife, the other half to his children." Father took a deep breath, like he was steeling himself. "The thing is that since the children are minors, the judge will appoint an executor to protect their interests."

The bile rose in my throat. "I'm their mother. I can protect their interests."

"I know. But be that as it may, the executor—or likely, executors, given the size of the ranch—will have a say in the sale of any property or assets."

"So I'll have to get their approval to sell my ranch?"

"I'm sorry, my dear."

Father wouldn't look at me. There was something he wasn't saying.

"Who will these executors be?" I asked.

"People who know the estate," Father said quietly. "Men from the county. Neighbors."

"Neighbors?" I said, furious now. "Like Kiel?"

Father didn't answer.

"He and his men killed Archibald! How can they have a say in this?"

I thought Father would say that it wouldn't happen. Those murderers would be hanging from a tree somewhere. Instead, he shrugged. "It's the law," he said.

The blood was pounding in my ears.

"Don't upset yourself, Helen. Just take things one day at a time."

I turned on him. "You'll stay to help me run the ranch," I said, hating myself for how desperate I sounded.

"I'm sorry, Helen. I can't leave my business for that long."

"But how will I manage, with no husband or kinfolk?" My voice was high. I willed myself not to cry.

"You're strong, my dear. You'll figure this out."

I bit my lip so hard that I tasted blood. Somehow, I'd see this through. I owed it to Archibald and my children to be strong.

After that, Father went off with Santiago to see a new foal. I wandered out to the kitchen garden. Nipe and the other women were curing jerky over a fire, the thin cuts of beef hanging down in strips. Archibald had promised a huge order to the mining company in El Dorado. We'd already slaughtered the cows. I guessed Nipe and the others had decided we couldn't let the meat go to waste.

El Dorado was a morning's ride. We'd load up the jerky. One of the ranch hands could drive me. With all those hungry miners, the owners wouldn't refuse the meat, even if it was me selling it. With that money, I'd buy feed for the herd and whatever else Santiago said we'd need to get through the fall.

I walked out to the arbor. The grape vines were heavy with fruit. Soon, there'd be grapes to pick and wine to make. My Paiute friends would help me, as they had last year. When the pumpkins and squash and corn came in, we'd harvest them together. I looked out to the fields, where the golden wheat swayed in the breeze. We'd been careful to keep it well-irrigated. There would be a bumper crop.

There would be food for me and mine: my children, Nipe and the rest of my Paiute neighbors, the ranch hands and cowboys. We'd lay in a winter crop. Potatoes. Lettuce. Maybe asparagus. Off in the distance, the cattle grazed. I could almost hear the hammering of hooves and the yeehaws of the cowboys. There was some grazing land to the west that was for sale.

Father and I would buy it together, just to be sure there wasn't any question about ownership. Our herds would grow. Los Vegas Rancho would thrive. When it came time to sell, we'd make more money than even Archibald would have imagined.

People were always coming and going from this land. First, the settlers, who sent word east about the spring and

15

encouraged others to follow. Then the Mormons, fired up with religious fervor and greed, who built adobe huts and dug silver mines, all the while promising paradise to the Paiutes, whom they enslaved. They'd fled after drought and dissension had divided their ranks.

Now the farmers and the railroad men, who tried to bend the land to their will.

This place was supposed to be temporary for me, too. A waypoint in the travel back to Pony Springs or someplace else. But standing there that day, I felt a kinship with those who came and didn't leave: the Mexican cowboys and hands who'd come from villages just beyond the southern borders. The Paiutes, who'd learned to live in this seemingly inhospitable place, and who, even now, refused to be forced out.

I could be like them. This could be home. At least for now.

I went out to the corral to find Santiago. We needed some new doors.

––––––––––

Suzanne Samuels writes about the experiences of people caught in unexpected and unwanted situations who must find a way forward. Her award-winning fiction and nonfiction, which includes stories, essays, and poems, have been published in numerous journals and anthologies. Her nonfiction books and articles on law and society have received widespread acclaim. After spending most of her life in the New York City area, Suzanne moved to the Adirondack Mountains in New York in 2020. Her debut historical novel, *Seeds of the Pomegranate*, will be published in fall 2025; her second book, *The Orphans' Wheel*, will follow in fall 2027.

Cowboy Justice

Sally Milliken

Dare to do right,
Dare to be true,
Dare to do good
Everything will come right for you.

—*Helen J. Stewart,*
in a letter to her youngest child, Archie Jr.,
not long before he died in a tragic accident
at age fourteen (in 1899)

WILL STEWART FELT AS IF HE'D JUST closed his eyes. He groaned and rolled over on the hard ground, away from the rock that had kept him awake most of the night.

His brother Hiram nudged him again with his boot and growled, "It's time."

Will stretched to loosen his tight muscles. He blinked the dust out of his eyes and scratched his mustache and chinstrap beard. He heard the nearby yip of a coyote over the sound of wind through the Las Vegas Valley. Several bats flitted overhead.

The mountains surrounding the valley were looming shadows. The sun would not rise over them in the October sky for several hours, but the moon was only three days past full and gave them enough light for their purposes.

Hiram was already packing his saddlebags. They'd both checked to be sure their guns were fully loaded before they'd gone to sleep. His brother checked his rifle again and readjusted his Stetson. When Hiram was wearing the hat, he looked younger than twenty-five, with his clean-shaven baby face. Without a hat, his bald head shone bright as a wet rock, making him look years older.

"Hiram, Hi—slow down." Will sat up and pulled on his flat-brimmed Stetson hat. "I thought we were going tomorrow

17

night." Will adjusted the collar of his dark flannel long-sleeved shirt—the same as Hiram's—and brushed the dust from his dark duck pants as he stood. He'd slept in his worn leather boots.

He'd promised Hiram years ago that they'd have their chance to avenge their father. Hiram didn't know it, but Will had also promised their mother and sisters he'd prevent Hiram from doing anything rash.

"Change of plans. I scouted the ranch." Hiram inspected his Colt revolver. "I heard shouting. The boys are alone, and they're drunk."

Will scoffed. "Aren't they usually?"

"If we're in luck, they're already passed out." Hiram took a swig from a tin cup, wiped his mouth with the back of a hand, and pointed toward a second cup on a rock. "There's Arbuckle's for you."

Will rolled his blanket and prepared his horse. He returned to where his brother waited by the remains of the campfire. The cold coffee was bitter and so thick he nearly had to chew it. He added a splash of whiskey.

They reviewed their plan even though they'd gone over it too many times to count. They'd been discussing various options for years, ever since their father had been killed in an ambush at Kiel Ranch sixteen years before. Will had been ten, Hiram eight. As the eldest, Will felt responsible for his younger sibling. Hiram was the more reckless of the two, and Will had spent most of his life encouraging him to think before he acted. So far, that had kept him—both of them—alive.

Hiram hissed as he warned, "Once we reach the edge of the ranch, no talking."

Will grunted into his cup. "I know."

Hiram's eyes darted around as he scanned the area. He dumped the remainder of his coffee into the dust and said, "You shouldn't have anything to do with this. You're not a good liar."

Will followed him to the horses. They were restless, as if sensing his unease. "Don't worry about me. I'll do what needs to be done." Will thought about Hiram's wife and baby. "And I have less to lose."

Holding on to the reins, Will grabbed the saddle horn, stepped into the stirrup, and settled on the saddle. They rode side by side toward the Kiel Ranch, one of three ranches— their family's being the largest—within Las Vegas Valley. They'd traveled the same route hundreds of times.

They startled a jackrabbit, which darted across the trail toward a Joshua tree. They were only a handful of miles from their family's property. Their mother and sisters, and Hiram's wife and child, would be safely in bed, unaware of what they were about to do.

He focused on the sound of the horses breathing and the soft clop of hooves in the sand. He flinched at the sharp sound of his horse's hoof hitting a rock, imagining the feeling of a bullet hitting his chest. He guessed they had a fifty-fifty chance of success. He swallowed the dust in his throat.

The line of citrus trees announced they were close to the homestead area. The cottonwoods along the creek had already lost their leaves for the winter. Hiram and Will led their horses around the sheep pen. The faint smell of moisture from the natural spring tickled Will's nose and made him thirsty.

Under the cover of the trees, Hiram held up his hand. Will reined his horse to a stop.

Hiram unwrapped two horseshoes from the saddle horn and attached one to the bottom of each of his boots. He slid off his horse and then held Will's horse as Will tied horseshoes on his own feet. Hiram checked that the straps were tight before Will dropped to the ground.

Hiram tied the reins to a low branch and shoved a rifle into Will's hands. He grabbed his own rifle and patted his Colt at his side. Will tucked his revolver at his waist and checked for extra ammunition.

Walking on the horseshoes was awkward at first, but Will quickly got the hang of it. They'd practiced and he knew it would work, but he looked behind himself anyway. When the dust settled, all he saw were hoofprints in the sand. No one would ever know they'd been there. As long as they survived. And there were no unexpected witnesses. The Kiel brothers often hosted an assortment of outlaws, so anything was possible. Will trusted that Hiram's scouting was accurate, but situations changed faster than a hand on a quick draw.

Will followed Hiram along the line of trees. He was so focused on not making a sound that when Hiram halted, Will ran into his back.

He took a step back and scanned the small adobe house fifty feet away. The building was dark, and the light of the moon danced off the wooden shingles. Will glanced at his brother and followed his lead. Hiram held up a hand again.

Will flattened himself against a tree. The last view of Hiram before he slipped away was the glow of his eyes and the white of his teeth as he grinned.

A horse whinnied and snorted, and Will held his breath and froze. He heard the animal shuffle and then nothing. He counted to twenty and started breathing again.

Hiram made the low sound of an owl hooting. It was time.

Hiram fired the first shot through a front window. They heard shouting, and the front door flew open.

The Kiel brothers must have sobered up fast. One of them yelled as he burst out of the house, his head lowered.

Will recognized the voice. "William," he whispered to himself. They shared a name but little else. Will was a pillar of the community, involved with multiple civic organizations. He was a proud and sharp contrast to William Kiel. Most law-abiding residents steered clear of that William.

Hiram fired his rifle, and Will followed a split second later. Preparing his body for the recoil from the rifle was second nature. The acrid smell of burnt powder was familiar.

William stumbled and fell to the ground out of view. Did they hit him?

Hiram appeared next to him.

"Where's Ed?" Will whispered.

Hiram ducked behind another tree trunk as a shot came from the window. "That answers that." He peered at the house.

"He won't be able to see well from there." Will fired toward the house. "Keep firing with both guns. I'll go around back."

Will reloaded and fired his rifle. He moved ten feet away and then took a shot with the revolver.

Hiram disappeared. He heard one shot. And then all was quiet.

The sun was beginning to lighten the sky, revealing the layer of smoke lingering around the house. A woodpecker—woken up by the noise and the light—began to hammer.

Hiram appeared in the open doorway. "All clear," he called. Will looked around and exhaled with relief. They needed to work quickly, just in case someone had heard the noise.

Will bent to pick up his empty rifle cartridges. Despite Hiram's assurance, Will approached the house slowly with his revolver drawn. William lay in a ditch thirty feet from the house. The tip of a rifle was visible near his shoulder. He checked his pulse. Nothing. Will left him there. Better him than me, he thought.

He entered the house through the front door and saw Ed on the floor near the open window, blood pooling near his head. Hiram checked Ed's revolver—he'd gotten more than one shot off, and that was all they needed—then placed the revolver in his right hand, curling his fingers around the handle.

Will found Ed's rifle. He placed it across the doorstep as if it had been dropped in a rush. Hiram removed spent cartridges from his pocket and scattered them nearby.

"We need to get out of here." No one had arrived, but they didn't want to push their luck.

The sun rose higher over the Las Vegas Range. They followed their tracks and returned to their horses. Will was relieved to remove the horseshoes from his feet.

Hiram looked back. No one was following them. He shoved his rifle in his saddlebag and glanced at Will. "We did it." Hiram's smile was as wide as Will had ever seen, as if he'd been holding it in since the day their father was killed. He pumped his fist. "We did it—"

Will nodded and sagged against his horse. Twenty-two residents were now twenty. How did he feel? Will knew it wasn't over yet. If they were caught, tougher times were just beginning.

Hiram glanced at Will as he stowed the horseshoes in his saddlebag. "Mother cannot know. She is too respected in town."

"She'll guess. You know she will."

"It doesn't matter. If anyone asks, she can honestly say that she had nothing to do with it."

"Could be days before anyone discovers them. And when that happens, they'll suspect us."

"Well, if the opportunity strikes, you should be the one to find the bodies. Not me." Hiram wiped his forehead with a handkerchief. "People in town will believe you."

They rode west in silence back to their campsite before turning toward home, adding a detour through a corner of Jim Wilson's Sand Stone Ranch. They passed a herd of cattle, and Hiram waved his hat at a man fixing a fence post. If asked, it would look like they were returning from delivering fruit and vegetables to miners below Red Rock Canyon.

Will frequently turned around to see if anyone was following them. He felt his shoulders relax as they rode northeast back to their ranch along the Las Vegas Creek. Home.

**

Around the family dinner table that night, their mother, Helen, announced, "There's a delivery for Kiel Ranch. Who's available tomorrow?" As postmistress, she often made such requests.

Will flicked a glance at Hiram and then quickly volunteered. "I'll go."

She nodded. "First light. And Frank," she lifted a finger toward their longtime ranch hand, "You go, too."

***

Three days later, Will worked in the vineyard, fixing a grape trellis that had fallen over and cleaning dead leaves and debris from under the plants. As his mother had requested, he and Frank had ridden to Kiel Ranch. They'd seen vultures circling overhead as they neared. Will had let Frank go first. The bodies of William and Edwin Kiel had been as they'd left them, except the flies and animals had also arrived. Hiram would have been impressed at how surprised Will responded to finding the bodies. Frank did not suspect a thing.

Will took a break from his work with the vines and stopped for a swig of water under the shade of a cottonwood.

"Did they believe that it was a murder-suicide?" Will's mother's voice startled him. His heart pounded so hard it felt like it would burst from his chest. He looked around. No one was there. Who was she talking to? He caught a glimpse of two people sitting on a bench by the creek. Not wanting them to hear him, he pressed himself closer against the tree and tried to slow his breathing to hear better.

Frank responded. "So far."

"What did you tell the judge and the coroner's jury?"

"What we saw. That Will and I went to the ranch at your request to tell the Kiels that their wagon wheels had arrived. We found the door of the house wide open and went to investigate. We yelled, but there was no answer. We first found Edwin—shot in the head—in the kitchen, clutching his Colt. We looked around and found William outside with his shotgun, partially in a ditch, as if he'd been surprised by his brother. The judge didn't ask as many questions as he could have. The evidence was good enough for him, and likely he was afraid of the answers. Besides, people are happy to be rid of them."

"What if Will and Hi face accusations? Or worse, are arrested?"

"How could they be? Your sons were delivering supplies to the miners, miles from there. And as you planned, I was a witness to finding the bodies. Everything appeared aboveboard." There was a pause. "You know I'd do anything for you."

Will held his breath. He wanted to lean closer but didn't dare move.

"Things had gotten more and more tense between the Kiels," his mother said. "That's what makes murder-suicide believable."

Frank murmured his agreement. "True. We've all seen it. Heard them going at each other."

"I have something to admit," his mother said. Will edged closer. He had to hear more. "I might have helped that along."

What was she talking about? thought Will. Frank said something he could not hear. Luckily, it didn't matter.

"I started rumors that William was hiding profits from Edwin. Then I followed up with a few well-timed letters—I am the postmistress after all. I forged and forwarded a few messages delivered from their suppliers, including references to missing payments. I also added numbers to bills to make it look like money was owed."

Will sat up.

Frank responded how Will would have. "You did what?"

Their mother had known they'd avenge their father. And she'd helped. Of course she had. Will shook his head in amazement at her strength. And cunning.

"It wasn't hard. It was mostly true anyway; I just sped up the timeline." His mother added, "The Kiels deserved what they got. I feel like I can breathe for the first time since Archie died, although I still have work to do. Everyone connected to

Archie's death has not been held accountable. Not yet. Our former ranch hand Schuyler Henry is next."

"I can see why, since Schuyler set everything in motion. He insulted you, knowing full well that Archie would never let that stand. And he didn't."

"My foolish husband took the bait, rode over, and got himself killed. Damn Schuyler—"

"You never believed the story, when the coroner's jury ruled he acted in self-defense?"

She scoffed. "Were they going to believe me—a woman— over the word of a man? Not likely. Not much has changed. Maybe someday, but not yet. No one else was there to witness what happened, and my word wasn't good enough. But I'll show them."

"What are you going to do?"

"I'm not sure yet. I've learned to be patient. Maybe facilitate a hanging, like with Hank Parrish."

"You had a hand in that, too? You never said. I'm impressed."

"The deaths can never lead back to my family."

"We'll make sure of it. Helen, when this is over, will you finally marry me?" Frank asked. "I've been more than patient."

His mother laughed, almost a giggle. Will wasn't used to hearing her make the sound. Or not for a very long time anyway. That was the last bit of convincing he needed that he and Hiram had done right, for her and their family.

The murmur of their voices disappeared as she and Frank walked up the creek toward the house. Will smiled. A light rain began to fall. It was such a rare occurrence that Will lifted his face to the sky and let the drops wash over him.

Author's Note: William and Edwin "Ed" Kiel died in October 1900. Their deaths were recorded as a murder-suicide. In the mid-1970s, their bodies were exhumed, and scientists determined from the remains that they were both murdered. No one knows who killed them, although some believe that

Will and Hiram "Hi" Stewart were responsible, hiding their presence by tying horseshoes to their boots, as imagined in this story. In 1902, the Stewart family sold part of their ranch land to the San Pedro, Los Angeles, and Salt Lake Railroad, and the land was later sold to become Las Vegas. The Kiel heirs followed in 1903. Helen and Frank married in 1903. Hiram died the same year. Las Vegas officially became a city in 1905. Will lived until 1931. For a time, Helen was the largest landowner in the county. She became known as the "First Lady of Las Vegas."

Sally Milliken writes contemporary and historical mysteries and crime fiction. Besides finding creative ways to bring villains to justice, she enjoys bending clay to her will on the pottery wheel and shooting pucks on net with her ice hockey team. Her stories have been published in various anthologies and online, including *Stone's Throw* and *Punk Noir*. She is working on her first novel, a historical mystery set in 1882 Massachusetts.
Find her at sallymillikenauthor.com or @sallyhistorymystery. Sally is a member of Sisters in Crime, Sisters in Crime NE, SinC Guppy Chapter, MWA, and the Short Mystery Fiction Society.

One of Our Own

Leah Moyes

August 1929
Las Vegas, Nevada

MELODY SWIPED THE BACK OF HER HAND across her moist forehead. Her shingle cut had lost some rigidity beneath the dimly lit incandescent lights and the sweltering heat of a crushing crowd. The sultry redhead slid up to the mic and ran her hands down the sides of her tight-fitting attire—a silver, tubular flapper dress that shimmered spectacularly at just the right angle. Pressing her lips together, she waited for the opening beats of "I'll See You in My Dreams" to begin. The measured vibration of Johnny's saxophone wailed, followed by Ricky's magic fingers at the piano.

The Gus Kahn and Isham Jones hit topped the charts four years ago and swiftly became one of Melody's favorites, especially since landing this gig in what was becoming one of the most sought-after nightclubs in Las Vegas, Nevada, the Oasis Café.

Melody's lips curved into a sly smile as she sang of long days and delightful dreams while couples swayed to the leisurely beats on the upper dance floor. Catching Nico's wink from the bar, her smile broadened for the handsome Italian from New Jersey and the memory of their recent first kiss.

The bright, blinking lights of E.P.'s newest sign flashed through the window and momentarily dazzled her. Melody's

27

boss, Mr. E.P. Bihlmaier, blazed a pioneer's trail of sorts—one of the first businessmen to not only take a chance on the inexperienced nineteen-year-old, but also follow the lead of the Overland Hotel in taking a plain sign and lighting it up like a Christmas tree.

The newest phenomenon drew every eye to Fremont Street, and, within days, the club's upper floor filled with patrons curious to see what such a display signified. Melody's sudden success stemmed from the growing crowd, and although she kept her focus, her heart fluttered through all six songs of her set before Lovely Lila took the stage behind her.

Like a gentle wind chime in a summer breeze, the final notes purred from Melody's lips and the room erupted in applause. Taking a deep breath, she stepped aside and gestured for the musicians to take a bow. In her mind, they truly deserved all the recognition.

"Hey, doll," Nico called from the bar as Melody descended the steps. Nicholas Strata, in his sharp silk shirt and pressed vest, had curly black hair that consistently fought for freedom beneath his stylish fedora. One day, Melody promised silently, she would be able to run her fingers through that hair, but for now she would settle for gazing into his eyes when time allowed. "You're the bee's knees, Mel. What can I get ya?"

Melody inched her dress upward and slid onto the stool. "Club soda, baby."

Despite Prohibition laws, the right words and ample cash could procure all manner of bootleg shine, especially here so close to Block 16 and the red-light district, but Melody didn't drink—not since that dreadful night one month ago.

When Nico smiled, the dimple in his right cheek deepened, causing Melody's heart to skip a beat, wondering how she got so lucky. This small-town girl from Paradise, Kansas, got on a train to nowhere and ended up singing at the Oasis Café in Las Vegas. Pinching her arm, she bit her bottom lip to keep her cry silent. Yep, it's real, she assured herself.

When Nico returned with her glass, two ice cubes bobbed on top. Leaning forward, he brushed his lips across her cheek on the way to her ear. "Can I walk you home tonight?"

Goosebumps rippled across her arms as his breath warmed her skin. "Uh-huh," was all she could manage. She only lived two doors down above the corner cigar shop, but she didn't care to tell him that. He'd find out soon enough.

"I can drift at midnight," he said, glancing over at a customer waving him down. "Can you stick around?"

She just managed to nod a yes when Beverly, her roommate, appeared at her side, hiding her face with one hand. "Mel, got a minute?"

"Sure.

As the women moved away from the bar, Melody caught sight of Beverly's smudged eyeliner under the muted lights. "What's wrong, Bev?" Melody had only known the woman for three weeks. They met at the train station and found a room to rent together. Beverly worked at the Billiard Room, half a block down, selling cigarettes.

"I, uh," she kept her hand over the left side of her face.

"I can't hear you," Melody cried and tugged Beverly's hand down, revealing an inflamed bruise on her cheekbone. "What happened?"

Beverly trembled, pressing a finger against Melody's lips. "Not so loud."

"Tell me," Melody demanded.

"I talked back."

"To whom?"

"Just some guy."

"Where?"

"Work."

"And he smacked you?"

"W-well," she stuttered. "I deserved it."

Melody's cheeks warmed. "No way, Bev. Nobody deserves that. What's he look like?"

"It's nothin', Mel. Leave it be. I only need the key to the apartment. I'm goin' home early."

"Not without me."

Beverly peered down at her hands. "I don't want no trouble, and this guy…he's swimmin' in it."

"Okay, kitten." Melody wrapped an arm around her friend. "Let's go." She led her down the stairs, through the café, and outside. She didn't have time to tell Nico about her change in plans, but he would understand. He was the kindest man she'd ever met, and that was saying something.

Paradise, the tiniest dot on the Kansas map, burst with kind men—all twenty-six of them over eighteen and under thirty, but somehow Melody latched on to the worst of them. There'd be a dozen charming gentlemen in a room, and Melody would end up going home with the liquored-up loser in the corner.

Just walking the thirty steps or so to their apartment door, Melody was reminded of the heat the Nevada desert produced from the sticky layer of perspiration that now coated her skin. Though her original plan entailed a stop for a day or two before catching another train and possibly taking a shot at Hollywood, it was E.P. 's blasted sign that called out to her. It lit up the moment she stepped off the train, and, like a lighthouse in a storm, it navigated her to safety. Though it took Melody another two days and a box of stogies to convince E.P. to give her an audition, she hadn't even finished Margaret Young's song "Oh! By Jingo! Oh By Gee!" when he hired her on the spot and, unbeknownst to him, saved her life.

Edging her dress up past the fringe, Melody retrieved her key from the inner folds of the white lace garter that hugged her thigh and unlocked the door. Inside, she felt her way to the pendant lamp and turned the knob just enough to fill the cozy space with some necessary light. Two small beds hugged opposite walls, sharing a small bed stand in between. The combination of sweet and spicy cigar aroma lingered in all the crevices of the room, including their bedding, clothes, and occasionally their hair, but the seventeen dollars the girls paid for monthly rent made the inconvenience worth it.

Melody gently clasped Beverly's arm and guided her over to the small washstand. They shared a toilet with the store but could only access it during open hours. From dusk to dawn, they used the bedpans tucked beneath their wooden bed frames.

Pouring water from the pitcher into the basin, Melody dipped the corner of a linen inside and squeezed the excess water out. Turning her friend to face her, she nudged Beverly's chin upward just enough to wipe the tears away, although nothing could be done about the bluish hue that formed on her cheekbone...nor the emotional pain that accompanied it. Melody knew that feeling all too well, and as she brushed the wet linen along her friend's skin, she couldn't help the deluge of memories that flooded her mind.

"C'mon, baby," Pete cried. "It won't happen again." The burly six-foot-two truck driver tried to pull Melody out from behind his kitchen table, where she huddled in the corner. "You know it ain't just me gettin' ugly with the fire sauce. You were, too." When he tried again, she flinched.

Clenching a wooden chair in his hands, he hurled it against the wall and it splintered into a hundred pieces, then he hollered, "Why do you make me hurt you? I want to love you, but you're just so damn stubborn!"

"Melody?"

Oh. Yes. She blinked repeatedly, trying to recall her last logical thought. "Uh-huh?"

"I think I'm good now." Bev stepped away and crawled into bed, pulling the light quilt her mother had stitched for her over her head.

Gripping the linen towel, Melody sat on the edge of her own bed, reflecting on that last night she spent in Kansas. Truth be told, she had tipped a few too many drinks but justified her relationship with the creep because "sober Pete" was a good guy. She shivered as thoughts of that night surfaced and the painful flashes of his shiny cowboy boot belt buckle...

31

Melody shook her head and tossed the towel toward the water basin. Never again! She'd worked too hard to let such fears destroy her. Now that the Oasis had given her a new life and opened the door for a career, she refused to let Pete, or any other louse, hold her back.

The next night when Melody entered the Oasis, Nico rushed to meet her at the door. His hair appeared wildly in disarray without his hat, and though his wrinkled silk shirt poked out past his suspenders, he appeared ruggedly handsome.

"Hey, doll, what happened last night?" He took Melody by the hand and led her to a private table in the corner, and as he sat down, he tugged her onto his lap. She struggled to concentrate as he put one hand on her thigh and caressed circles into her back with his other hand.

"Sorry, Nico," Melody said. "Bev had some trouble at the pool hall last night. I walked her home. I didn't want her to be alone."

Nico nodded. "Anythin' I can do?" Then he quirked an eyebrow in such a charming way that she couldn't help but smile in return. She considered his offer but hoped it never came to that; that this strange man who hurt Bev—not unlike Pete, Frank, or Jack from Melody's past—need not be reminded on how to treat a lady properly.

Melody cupped his cheek and felt the silky, smooth sensation of his recent shave and leaned in, pressing her lips against his. "No, handsome, but thank you."

He reacted by wrapping his arms around her and deepening the kiss.

"Hey, you two!" E.P.'s gruff voice rose from across the room, and despite the presence of several customers dining in the café, he hollered for their attention. "Let's go! Upstairs! People are arriving for the show."

Melody hopped off Nico's lap and giggled, touching her slightly swollen lips. She couldn't imagine a better way to begin her night. Approaching E.P., she patted his arm and winked.

The man may be tough on the outside, but he was undeniably a teddy bear on the inside and Melody knew how to soften him up. "Full house tonight, E.P.?"

He glanced down at the small ledger that he carried. "More than last night, sweetheart. Think you can handle it?"

"You got it, boss." She leaned forward and kissed his cheek. "I love your swanky sign, by the way. It lights up all of Fremont, and I bet you can see it from all over town."

He lifted his chin a notch and tugged on his suitcoat lapels with pride. "I think you're right, little lady." He smiled wide. "And they're all comin' just to see you. In fact..." He pointed to a nearby table. "Come meet my friends. They're here for the show."

E.P. took Melody by the hand and led her to the center of the café where two men and a woman each enjoyed a hearty steak with a side of fried eggs.

"Good evening, Ferguson." E.P. dipped his hat. "This here's Miss Melody Brooks, the star of the show."

A pink blush tinged Melody's cheeks. While she always held her own, she never felt like she outshone the others.

"Ah, yes." The man E.P. called Ferguson stood to his feet, sharply dressed in a fitted suit and classy gray fedora. "I heard you're a canary, sweetheart."

Melody smiled and held out her hand to shake, but he lifted it upward and kissed her knuckles like a fine gentleman would. "I'm Jim Ferguson, and this lovely dish by my side is my wife, Vera." Melody smiled in the woman's direction.

The third member of their party, dressed in a copper's uniform, stood up. "Spud Lake, miss." He winked. "I'm the police chief in this town. You need anythin', you come see me, ya hear?"

The dining room clock suddenly chimed seven times, knocking Melody out of her reverie. "Oh, please pardon me, I must go. Nice to meet y'all."

"Likewise," said Spud.

As Melody quickly hustled toward the stairs, she turned and blew a kiss to Nico, who remained on the corner chair. As she took to the stairs, she heard Nico call out, "Hey, E.P., we got any more ginger ale in the storeroom?"

E.P. replied gruffly, "Go check yourself, barkeep. What do you think I'm payin' you for?"

Melody laughed the rest of the way up the stairs and slid through the smoky crowd just as the opening act, Mr. Tilley and his terrific trumpet, began his set. There would be one more entertainer after him, then Melody.

In the green room backstage, Melody sat in front of the mirror. With trembling hands, she reapplied her dark red lipstick and powdered her nose. It had been some time since she felt the jitters like this, and she didn't know why they rose tonight. This was Melody's twelfth performance here at the Oasis Café, but she'd been performing in talent shows and county fairs since she turned five years old.

Pressing her hands tightly together to force them still, she ruminated over the last twenty-four hours. Could this reaction be due to the whole conundrum with Beverly? Her bruise looked heaps worse this morning, all swollen and purplish-blue.

Once again, Melody's thoughts drifted back to Pete and how she tiptoed around his sleeping form and snatched a handful of bills from his wallet and a few of her belongings. Melody hitched a ride with a kind elderly woman who drove her to the bus stop the next town over. It took her three days, two bus changes, and a train to get to Las Vegas...and twice as long for the bumps and bruises to heal.

Now, three weeks later, Melody wasn't sure she wanted to leave Las Vegas and resume her trek to California, even after she sent a post home to her mama the first week telling her that Fremont Street was *just a stop*.

But she also knew that the farther away she got from Pete, the better.

"Melody?" Johnny nudged her. "Hey, sugar, you ready? We're up in five."

"Oh." She pinched her cheeks to spur a rosy color. "Yep, all good."

Melody followed Johnny and Ricky out the door and onto the stage. Stealing a deep breath, she peered over to where Nico leaned against the bar with his mischievous half-smile. Melody's heart thumped an extra beat just before she stepped up to the mic.

Tonight, she wore a glittering blue dress with two rows of black fringe and a daring hem that only reached mid-thigh. With a matching headband and a double strand of pearls, she felt confident and beautiful.

When the piano notes to Bessie Smith's "Downhearted Blues" began, Melody reached up and clutched the mic with both hands, letting the music flow naturally through her. The song reminded Melody of her mother and the enormous Edison disc phonograph in their living room. That very turntable was the sole reason Melody ended up on stage. She felt a deep connection to music, believing it was a part of her soul.

After she sang rousing songs by Ruth Etting, Josephine Baker, and Margaret Young, Melody took a short five-minute break and headed for the bar. This time, she didn't even need to ask Nico for her club soda; he had it ready for her when she arrived. "Here you go, doll." He winked but couldn't stay and chat. The number of customers at the bar had doubled. Many seemed to know the right words and possessed the right number of clams to get their gin, brandy, and whiskey.

"Melody." Beverly appeared beside her. She wore a forest-green bucket hat pulled low and sunglasses the size of owl eyes.

"How in the world can you see your way around with these dark things, silly?" Melody attempted to tug the glasses down.

Beverly smacked her hand. "Don't. He's here."

"Who's here?"

"The man…" she whispered with a terror-infused tone.

"What man?"

She grunted. "The man from last night." She pointed to her bruise.

A heat fired up in Melody's chest. "Where is he?" She felt a surge of protection for her friend.

"Over there," Beverly whispered, pointing into the crowd.

Well, that didn't help. Melody peered over to find her band members waving her back. "Gotta go, Bev. Keep an eye on him. I have a new friend that might put *him* behind the eight ball." Melody referred to Spud Lake, the copper she met.

Beverly nodded and slumped down on the bar stool. Melody patted her arm and hustled back to the stage, taking Ricky's hand as he guided her up the steps to the front of an enthused crowd. Two songs later and a song by Mamie Smith, she had the room hopping again, swaying and twirling to the music.

When Mel caught Bev's eye, she pointed toward a big fella standing in the corner shadows. Melody couldn't make out the color of his skin, hair, or eyes back there, but when she reached the chorus of "My Man" by Fannie Price, the fella stepped into the light and shot the canary a wicked scowl.

Pete!

Melody stumbled over the song's words. Curious eyes fell upon her as she tried to even recall what note came next.

Pete took several more steps forward. Melody's pulse raced and her breath stuttered. When she stopped singing altogether, the instruments went on without her.

Johnny whispered from behind. "You all right, sugar?"

Melody's mind spun. Suddenly she was in the front seat of the elderly woman's car in Kansas, wearing a bloodstained blouse, shaking like a leaf. "You all right, sugar?" the woman had asked.

Melody gasped and stepped away from the mic. Beads of perspiration trickled down her cheeks as the lights, the heat, and the sounds all smothered her. Melody turned and fled, running as fast as she could in her high heels, flying down the stairs to the café and out to the sidewalk.

Peering behind her, Melody dipped into a nearby alley, stopping only to take a breath, then huddled behind a garbage can. Though the stench of rotten food, urine, and ash should've forced her to leave, she feared being seen. Reaching down to unbuckle one of the straps on her shoe, Melody rose up to find Pete looming over her.

Her entire body shuddered. "Wh-what ya doin' here?"

He grabbed her by the hair, hauling her deeper into the alleyway as she stumbled with only one shoe. Though she tried to scream, no sound surfaced.

"You didn't say goodbye, darlin'," he growled. "Even after you helped yourself to my wallet."

"H-how did you—"

"Find you?" he finished her sentence. "Your mama." Pete threw Melody to the ground, and before she even hit the dirt, the back of his hand struck her cheek and knocked her sideways. Pete then went for the pearls, ripping the double strand from her throat, sending the beads scattering in all directions.

Stunned and terrified, Melody rubbed her inflamed skin and, for a moment, wondered if she would even survive this time. Crawling along the ground, she collapsed as Pete's foot thrust excruciatingly into her torso. *Crack!*

Melody felt woozy, and her sight blurred. She knew Pete's silhouette hovered over her when she spied his shiny belt buckle. She had *not* forgotten that belt buckle. Throwing her hands up to her face, she cried and pleaded, waiting for the sharp edges to embed somewhere in her skull. Just as he raised his arms, she heard a pop. Pete stiffened, groaned, then wilted to the ground at Melody's feet.

Rubbing her eyes free of tears, she saw the silhouette of a man standing behind Pete, holding something that still smoked. *A pistol?* Seconds later, Nico and Beverly appeared on each side of her. Nico lifted her up, pulled her to his chest, and carried her out of the alley. As they passed the man with the gun, Melody recognized him not as the lawman, but Jim Ferguson from the café.

Nico rushed back inside the Oasis with Melody in his arms. As they passed beneath that audaciously lit sign, she couldn't help but feel strengthened by its sight, as if it beckoned her home.

When Nico entered the café, E.P. ushered the two of them into his office. Nico laid Melody on the nearby couch and surveyed her injuries. Beverly rushed over and pressed a wet compress to her friend's cheek.

"Did ya know 'im?" Nico asked as his thick East Coast accent flared through his heightened anxiousness.

"He—" Melody couldn't form a logical sentence.

Beverly spoke up. "He's the same man who hit *me* last night. I guess he just likes to hit girls."

Melody's breath shuddered as she spoke, "Y-yes, he hits girls," she managed to say. "And he's m-my former boyfriend."

E.P. waved Mr. Ferguson inside the room. She no longer saw the gun in his hands. He approached her with furrowed brows. "You copacetic, sweetheart?"

Melody sniffled. "Is Pete d-dead?"

"Now, don't you worry that pretty little head of yours. Spud's on it," Mr. Ferguson placated. "We take care of our own, darlin', and you, my dear, are one of our own."

Melody inhaled deeply, then closed her eyes.

When she opened them again, she felt the familiar comforts of her own bed above the cigar shop. Daylight streamed through the window as Nico slept nearby, leaning his head against the side of her bed. Melody maneuvered to a seated position and nudged Nico's shoulder. He mumbled, then shook awake, jumping to his feet and to Melody's side. Brushing her hair off her face, he kissed her forehead. "How ya feelin', doll?" He smiled that swoon-worthy grin.

Melody smiled back. "Much better."

Nico took her hand. "Thank goodness Mr. Ferguson found you. I can't imagine what would've happened if he didn't."

"Why did he?"

Nico tilted his head. "You don't know?"

"Know what?"

"He's the big cheese round here." Nico chuckled. "Nothin' gets past him."

Melody smiled as she recalled the gentleman's words from the night before. *You, my dear, are one of our own.*

"So now that this trouble is behind you, Mel, any chance you'll stay? Stay here with me?"

Melody ran her fingers through Nico's curls and beamed. "Seems like I've got a family here, Nico. Why on earth would I leave?"

Leaning over, he kissed her in a way that made her forget Pete, Kansas, and the cowboy boot belt buckle. Melody had found where she belonged, and who would've thought it would be an Oasis in the desert.

Leah Moyes is a wife, a mother, a lifelong student with a background in anthropology and history, and the author of over a dozen novels, including her award-winning *Berlin Girl Series* (finalist in Book Excellence and Reader's Favorite under the original name of *Berlin Butterfly Series*) and its prequel, *The Polish Nurse*, (Winner of Book Excellence under the original name of *Before Berlin*). Between writing and archaeological digs, her travels have helped her discover unique locations, cultures, and people for her historical fiction novels. Leah's website: www.leahmoyes.com.

Lady Luck

Laura Mace

November 1932
Black Canyon of the Colorado, site of the future Hoover Dam

SHOUTS OF MEN and the growl of machinery reverberate through the canyon. Nine days ago, the diversion tunnels opened to swallow the glittering Colorado River.

Oliver Cowan thumps the dust from his pants and hops through the leather belt of his climbing harness. He is working from a platform on the face of the canyon today, six hundred feet above the naked mud of the riverbed.

Oliver's rappel is a dance with gravity and stone. Down, down, down into the vertical world, he swings from ledge to arête to crevice. He scrapes away loose rock remaining from yesterday's jackhammer pass, smoothing any remaining features with his chisel and pickaxe.

A wail echoes through the grind of machinery. Oliver squints into the blindingly blue sky, picking out a strange dark shape below the jagged rim of the canyon.

He makes a wild swing to his left and seizes the falling man's leg with both hands. The momentum of the catch whirls them wildly away from the face, then back into the rock with a crunch. His harness feels like it will cut him in half.

"COWAN!" His foreman scrambles from the platform down to the thinnest of ledges. A hefty man, he moves with surprising speed to shove the dangling men against the wall,

41

halting their pendulous sweep. The hemp rope creaks as their feet scuffle for purchase—this section is already smoothed to virgin rock.

The high scalers on the platform shout encouragement as they fling ropes to the foreman, who loops one around himself and edges along the ledge. The fallen man clambers onto Oliver's shoulders so the foreman can help him into a harness.

Willing hands haul the three men slowly to safety. Everyone is suddenly grateful for his breath.

"Amazing, Cowan!"

"God..." The man who fell sags, then forces himself upright to pant a thank-you. "M-my name's Rutledge, Bureau engineer. I lost my grip up there during...inspection...injured my damn hand yesterday." Oliver feels a bandage on one of the hands wringing his own.

On their return to the station on the rim, men run to them from all over the site. Other high scalers cut through the crowd to pound Cowan's back. Of all the workers at the dangerous site, it's a feat they alone can admire viscerally. Surrounded by sunburned smiles, Cowan's own wide grin spreads bashfully over his broad face.

"Thank God," the rescued inspector keeps saying. "Thank you—Cowan, is it? I'd be dead in the mud if it wasn't for you."

***

That evening, Oliver is allowed to shower in the Boulder City barracks and dine in the managers' mess. He downs three helpings of roast beef between handshakes and attaboys.

"Wait till the papers get wind of it!" The headman of the entire project, Frank Crowe, shakes Oliver's hand—after chastising the engineer who fell, of course.

Natives cannot live in the Boulder City camp, so Oliver makes his way along the road back to the shantytown where he sleeps. His eyes are drawn to the shining points of the Hunters following the Great Bear, so sharp in the desert night. Rising to the northeast, the Salmon calls his thoughts homeward.

***

Oliver's uncle was the best fisherman in the family. It was not for anything he knew—knowledge was passed like steaming coffee on a misty morning. No, he was the best because he got right into the salmon runs. His dexterity and rope work got him to dizzying places that made the rest of the family laugh and shake their heads. Down into the Great Kettle Falls, say, a sacred place where the salmon strained upward through a river turned to white vapor. His uncle taught Oliver how to lash himself to their platform over the wild falls, how to balance and wrestle the ocean-strong fish from the most exposed current.

The best fisherman, that is, until Oliver grew up. Then his daring nephew wielded his pine pole net like a wild man, scaling the cliffs to fix a line over the falls so he could swing out and pluck salmon from the midst of the torrent. He fought his thrashing catch while dangling in midair. His uncle was proud of Oliver's skill. It was his legacy, for he had no children of his own.

"The river is my woman. I belong to her. I know her spirit, and she takes care of me." He said it in a dozen variations over the years as they gutted coho and mended nets. As they roasted their lunch catch in the potholes that gave the falls their name, Uncle told him ancient stories.

When the hard times came, Oliver and his cousins made their way to the Hoovervilles of the desert in search of work. They joined lines of would-be laborers stretching through shantytowns in one hundred and twenty-degree heat. They learned that no one would hire a man from the Colville tribe while white men stood in line…unless he could stomach the feat of lowering into the canyon every day to detonate and hammer away the surface rock. If the body could fly, skin didn't matter—and he'd make more money, too.

Oliver's rope skill and comfort in high places soon had him on the Six Companies' payroll, dangling three hundred, five hundred, a thousand feet above a doomed riverbed.

***

Headlights behind him flood the stars. Arnold Parks, the foreman from the rescue, leans out the rear window of a long-lined Chrysler.

"Get in, Cowan! Let's have a real celebration!" His portly face splits in a boyish grin.

"Fremont Street!"

"But...it's only Monday," Oliver laughs.

"We've got a day's leave—a thank-you from the Six." Parks tosses him a flask and opens the car door.

Grinning, Cowan ducks inside.

"Our hero, Oliver Cowan." Parks introduces him to the interior of the car. "This is T.J. Lindt, reporter with none other than the *New Yawk Times*—you've just given him his reward for driving out to this hellhole." The driver flashes Cowan a grin in the rearview mirror. "And Tom Wills, you know him, of course." Parks taps the shoulder of the man in the passenger's seat, the big boss of the scalers for Six Companies.

"Nice to meet you, fellas." Normally a talkative fellow, Oliver feels overwhelmed.

"Helluva thing, Cowan," says the reporter. "I've been kicking around here lookin' for a page-turner for ages. How ya feeling after your heroic rescue?"

"Shucks," says Oliver, "there wasn't anything heroic about it, it was just instinct."

"Tarzan of the Apes instinct," laughs Lindt. "I'll ask how you feel about it after a soda or two at the Sal."

"You been to Sal Sagev?" Parks asks. "Best cards in Nevada."

Oliver says nothing. It is forbidden for any Six Companies' employee to patronize Las Vegas. He has anyway, of course—high scalers crave risk in all its forms. But he's not about to fess up, even to other guilty parties.

The glittering Edison bulbs spelling "HOTEL Sal Sagev" form the brightest of the constellations of Las Vegas. A stately brick building on the corner of Fremont Street, the hotel radiates modernity, respectability. On a Monday night, only a few regulars grace the tables with their escorts.

Wills hails the bartender. "Whiskey soda here."

"Lindt here got us rooms," Parks says to Oliver, sliding a stack of chips across the table. "Says to enjoy ourselves."

The reporter introduces Oliver to a blond named Sandy and buys him a whiskey soda that bubbles comfortably beside the roast beef. After a couple more and a small win at the table, Oliver decides it is the most exciting night of his twenty-two years.

Alone in the hotel room in the wee hours, he no longer feels so satisfied. Accustomed though he is to swinging on ropes over five hundred feet of chasm, every muscle remembers the adrenaline and effort of the mid-air rescue. Like the contents of a sack snapped out of freefall, everything inside him has been jarred. He struggles to get comfortable on the overstuffed feather mattress, sweats under the green velvet coverlet. The twenty-four-hour lights of the hotel sign glare through the sheer curtains.

When he finally dozes off, he is falling again, but the air is sweet with the breath of trees. He dangles above his home river, eyeing the course of a June hog, the biggest coho salmon. He swings to meet its leap up the white rapids, but he realizes he has forgotten his pole. He reaches for the huge silver fish with both hands, hugging it close. As he clutches it to him, the scales turn to buckskin and flannel. His uncle.

Oliver smells the familiar smell of his body…then looks up. His rope is fraying, the rope, strand by strand…he and his uncle tumble together into the froth of Kettle Falls. Into the arms of his uncle's woman, who draws them, gasping, to her stony bed.

Oliver thrashes awake, still feeling the crushing weight of the water, his uncle in his arms.

A woman with long, dark hair sits silhouetted against the light of the hotel sign. Her legs are crossed under a bloodred duster, the only color in the darkened room. A cigarette glows below the brim of her hat.

Oliver fumbles for the lamp switch.

"Uh, you looking for someone, ma'am?" His mind jumps from prostitution to robbery to vengeance over his petty winnings.

"It's time for you to go home, Oliver." The voice is familiar, but he cannot place it.

Musical, deep, sad.

He sags back onto his elbows, feeling queasy. "I'm sorry, do I know ya?"

"I'm looking for a riverman," she says.

"Er, did someone pay you to come up here? What's your name?"

"These days, in this place?" She lifts the cigarette toward the sign. "When they murmur over their cards, blow on their dice—they call me Lady Luck." She takes a long pull, and Oliver smells mullein and sage mingled with the tobacco. "But I have many names—rain, runoff... salmon. I am the answer to the prayer. The blessing."

Oliver Cowan is only a generation or two from someone who would not blink at such a pronouncement, who might know how to answer, what to offer her. But he is far from home. He shakes his head, thinking he's just had too much to drink.

"You are here because you did a heroic thing," she says. "A lucky thing."

"Only what any of the fellas woulda done," he says for the tenth time that day.

She raises her hat brim and fixes him with a blazing gaze—eyes like sun on the water under a desert sky, flecked with green like willow branches trailing in the current. Her strong cheekbones are proud above a mouth hard with anger.

"What are you doing here, Oliver?" she asks. "Besides saving a life?"

"Making a living, like a man's gotta do." He rubs his eyes and yawns. Beneath the glee of his wildly fun job pulses guilt about leaving his family. It takes very little to bring it to the surface. "I make more than anyone back home," he says defensively. "Couldn't keep getting five cents a fish forever, not with the canned stuff comin' out of Alaska. We'd lose our land, the house. And the government isn't giving half the oil or flour ration they did before."

"Your uncle. He won't survive if it happens."

Now she has his full attention.

"He won't survive when the floodwaters come. When I'm drowned again in tunnels, trapped in another lake, when my children cannot come home from the ocean anymore. When I am choking on silt, he won't want to survive."

Oliver tries blearily to piece her meaning together. "You mean this dam?"

"Here? I have already lost. Nine days ago, I lost," she whispers.

What happened nine days ago? Oliver isn't even sure of the date. The woman is silent for a moment, blinking like she is fighting back tears.

"Luck lifted you out of that canyon today for a reason," she continues throatily. "You are free now—a hero. Go home, while the eyes of the country follow, and fight for me. Fight for your uncle and your river."

"Free? Fight? How?"

"You will know; you will have your chance."

She stands, red duster swishing above shining blue heels. The door does not click behind her. She has gone to weep icy tears on mountaintops, gush through high meadows, then drown in diversion tunnels with echoing sobs.

***

In the predawn of Wednesday morning, Oliver walks up the road to the post office in Boulder City to send a letter to his family. He isn't much of a writer and had to borrow stationery and a stamp. He eked out a few lines about the rescue and a promise to send a clipping from the paper when it came. He also asked for news of his uncle and the fishing grounds.

He drops the envelope in the night slot and tucks his hands into his jacket against the chill. The stars of the Leaping Salmon are fading in the west as he heads toward the canteen for some black coffee. He's sorting out the day's gear when he hears an unfamiliar voice rumbling through the morning chatter of the scalers.

"Where can I find Oliver Collins, sonny? The hero from Monday's rescue?"

"Cowan? He's yonder," says a stringy Southern boy, gesturing Oliver's way. A group of men in suits threads through the dusty climbers and their assorted tackle. At their head is a portly man in pinstripes who pumps Oliver's hand and doesn't let go.

"Well, there, my boy!" He says, popping an unlit pipe in and out of his lips with every sentence. "I was out on business Monday night, but I'm excited to meet ya. Elliot's the name. I'm the stock manager and press liaison for the Six Companies. You know Lindt, I think, and this here's Price, the Bureau's photographer."

"Say, Parks, Willis," he calls to the supervisors. "Can we borrow your boy today for some photographs? Great story for the dam here, great publicity, eh? The heroes on the front lines of progress."

Oliver puts on his harness and tar-sealed safety hat. They choose a site where the men in suits can stand comfortably and look across a little gap at Oliver as he settles into his bosun's seat. He's only lowering a few feet, but this morning he is much more aware of the chasm beneath him, thinking of the speed of the engineer's fall when he grabbed him.

"That's right, sonny, right there!" calls the photographer. Oliver leans back and grins his humble grin. The men in suits nod approvingly.

"He's got an easy way about him, eh, and you can't even tell he's Indian!" Elliot beams at Lindt. "We've got the reception for the hydroelectric stakeholders in Los Angeles; we've got to have him there!"

From this vantage, Oliver can also see over the cofferdams to the place where the blue of the river disappears into the new diversion tunnels. It has only been eleven days since the river was diverted—the floor of the canyon is still thick red mud.

"Give us a wave!" the photographer shouts. Oliver turns from the view and waves obediently at the camera.

"Why, this scenery, that smile, they ought to make a movie of it," Lindt the reporter laughs as Oliver pulls back up to the rim.

"What a gas that would be for Six Companies and the dam!" Elliot agrees. "Say, my boy, would you like to visit Los Angeles? We've got a gala in a few weeks for some stakeholders; we'll see to it you have a wonderful time!"

***

The publicity builds. His letter is still on its way to the Colville Reservation, but white relatives call from as far off as Minneapolis, where his aunt reads him the headline from the tribute—"Plucks the Falling Engineer Right Out of Mid-Air!" and demands all the details. He has to let her go to free the line for press calls.

But at night, as he lies in his hotel bed, smile wearier than his body, his dreams descend into another chasm, this one with the Columbia rushing below. He hears the words of the woman who called herself Lady Luck.

Go home and fight for me.

***

A long-lined Chrysler hums west along Highway 91 toward California. Oliver stares out the window at the red desert, excited as any young man would be, wearing a new suit and heading to the big city for the first time. He daydreams about what might come next—a car, perhaps money for a new house

49

back home. His future seems as open and clear as the road before him.

A woman in a red duster and wide-brimmed hat watches until the car vanishes over the horizon, then turns to walk north.

Sun glitters through the veil of mist that hangs around the falls. It is a green place, the air sweet with the breath of trees. When the river meets the new concrete of the Grand Coulee Dam, the rapids slowly climb the cliffs where Oliver Cowan learned to fish and to fly.

The water reaches an empty fishing platform where a pine salmon rod lies abandoned, its net empty. Oliver's uncle has left it there, his final prayer to Lady Luck.

Laura Catherine Mace lives by the largest river in southern Colorado, where she was born and eventually returned after seeking stories thither and yon. She teaches both yoga and history, drawing on these disciplines to breathe life into enduring legends. She is the author of *The Queen Maeve* trilogy and the mashup novel, *Saint George the Dragonrider,* as well as a nonfiction handbook, *The Yoga of the Seasons,* coming in early 2026. Her website is lauracmace.com.

A Hot Vegas

Sally Bays

Take two pieces of bread or a round hamburger bun. Butter two sides of the hamburger bun lightly.

Take a wiener and slice it up into thin slices and spread it over one side of the bread or bun.

Take two slices of well-fried bacon and cut or crumble them over the wiener.

Melt some strong cheddar cheese. Pour enough of it over to just nicely cover them. Salt and pepper to taste and serve at once.

Recipe for the Vegas sandwich
Bull Cook and Authentic Historical Recipes and Practices, 1960

"GIMME A HOT VEGAS, BILLY," SHE SAYS, the same way she's been saying it all week—thick with a drawl that hints of somewhere humid. With a sway to her hips, she slides up to the counter. Milk's has had a lot of lookers come through the doors since I've worked here, but this dame outclasses them all.

She came in first on Monday, wearing a red dress, soft fabric that caught the light of the sun reflecting off the front pane window. Most redheads couldn't pull off that color, but she made it look like one of our famous desert sunsets. The baubles on her ears told me maybe she was one of those gangster's girls, slumming it down this end of Fremont Street, but she's been back every day since.

"Coffee?" Damn if my voice doesn't squeak, though I've had a shadow on my chin half a decade now.

"Nah, honey, it'll stain my teeth," she says, just like Tuesday, when I'd gotten up the nerve to do more than hand her a menu, and Wednesday, when she'd asked me my name. She hasn't offered hers yet, probably figuring I should know it already.

She pulls out a silver case and fills the diner with a cloud of menthol. "Water'll be just fine."

"Classic Vegas or with my spin?" Yesterday, Thursday, she let me put a tomato slice between the bacon and cheese. My boss, Tony, doesn't have vision like that, but Tony takes the afternoons off to see his girl dance at the Flamingo, so it's been her and me all week.

"Classic, honey. And ice in that water? Sure is hot out today." She clears her throat, and again, then tucks her lips around the shaft of the cigarette, leaving cherry-bomb kisses on the white paper. My knees lose themselves a minute until she unclenches her mouth, and the cigarette finds its way back to the ashtray. My arm shakes as I set the water glass on the counter.

"Sticks and straw," Mother always says. "You're sticks and straw, Billy. Have another slice of pie." When I didn't get picked up for the football team. "You're just sticks and straw, Billy. You'd blow right off the boat even before you got to Germany." When the draft board sent me back even though I could shoot the eye out of a bighorn. "You're just sticks and straw, Billy; that girl would crush you half to death. You just stay on here with me." When Penny Gilbert wouldn't step out on a second date with me.

She sees I'm nervous as I wipe up the water-slosh with napkins pulled from the dispenser. "You're sure cute." The words slip out with a cloud of smoke. "I'll take care of that while you work on my sandwich. You know I like my weenies real thin."

The first time she made that joke, on Monday, I had to stand in the storeroom for five minutes. "Looking for buns," I'd told her, when I was composed again.

"Why, I got a nice set right here!" She'd laughed in her throat, and I'd excused myself again. It's Friday now, and I only blush.

"Presumption and sauce," Mother would say, but Mother isn't here, and I won't pick her up until after her shift at the courthouse, typing up and filing the wedding certificates and such. It would be hours yet before we shared our grilled cheese on toast and tin-can soup.

"You ever gonna ask me about myself?" She spins a little on her stool and stretches her legs so I catch a glimpse before I turn to my work. "I came to town a few months ago with my fella, now that he's left his wife official like. He's been around since during the war, trying to make something of it down here. He built me a place in Beverly Hills, if you can believe it. Beverly Hills. But he's been distracted, blond secretary kind of distracted, so I've been trotting around this dusty old place, and I'm half bored to tears."

Usually she doesn't talk, just watches me while I toast the bun, running her tongue over her teeth when she catches me glancing her way. Now her cigarette is moving faster, mouth to ashtray, ashtray to mouth.

"Can't imagine that secretary is as pretty as you." My voice cracks like a cold glass hitting hot water. But it earns me a smile that numbs the embarrassment.

She blows a smoke ring that fades like a target over my head. I get back to her sandwich. "Oh, it isn't the pretty that matters, it is the new. My fella likes a fresh girl; I was the fresh girl a couple years ago, but now that he has ditched his wife and girls, and bought me a mansion in the Hills, well, I'm not so fresh anymore."

I set an extra pickle on her plate. On Tuesday she ate her pickle first, watching me watch her in a way that made me think that she'd wanted more. I've made that mistake before though, and I don't want this to be a Penny Gilbert situation again. Not when she has a fella of the kind that can afford a mansion and all the girls he wants. Still, watching won't hurt.

"You going back to your mansion, then?" My damn hands shake again when I slide the plate in front of her.

She winds her fingers through mine, and I stop trembling, breathing, too. "I sure don't want to, not alone anyway. I hate being lonely." She leans close, close enough that I can see more than I ought down the front of her dress. Green today, with buttons up the front that end low. The fabric is thin enough to tell she isn't wearing a girdle like Mother, or whatever the contraption was that I tried to get off Penny Gilbert. "You don't want me to leave, do you, Billy?" She asks in a voice that sounds like melted butter and promises.

"No, ma'am." I pull my gaze back to her eyes, and she squeezes my hands again before taking up her cigarette. She looks over her shoulder as the bell on the door rings and an older woman comes in. The lady asks for a coffee and a slice of cherry pie, sitting in the far booth.

"Don't leave?" I ask as I pass behind the counter with the coffeepot. Not like when someone came in yesterday and she left most of her sandwich on the plate, the tomato turning the bottom bun sodden pink.

"Sure, honey." She picks up the pickle slice and winks at me.

I putter, ignoring the old woman's throat clearing and raised fingers after I drop off the thinnest slice of pie in the dish and half a cup of stale coffee, until she drops six bits on the table and leaves in a huff.

"Well, that isn't going to get you a return customer," she giggles, still not having touched her sandwich. "God, I hope I never get that old; no man would have me."

I choke on words I wish I could say, but I've never been the brave sort, and they sit halfway up my gullet.

"Not that my fella wants me now. Not that any fella would want me. I already have two wrinkles, see?" She purses her lips like she might lean over and kiss me.

"Hmmm, I don't see anything," I lie.

She leans forward again and tilts her neck so I can see everything down her dress again. "See? Right there." She points a lacquered nail to the lines snaking from the corner of her lips. "No wonder he's leaving me for a blond."

How the secretary's hair color plays into things is almost enough to distract me until her mouth starts quivering and pulls my attention back. "I'm going to be alone forever, Billy, alone! Why, I can't hardly take the thought of it! I'll be dead in a week, I'm sure."

Black mascara tears run a track down her cheek and if I were the brave sort I might wipe them away with one of the water-slosh napkins, but I'm Sticks and Straw Billy, so instead I refill her water glass and push it toward her a little.

Finally, I can't stand her crying. "There are a lot of fellas out there who would be real glad to have a dame like you on their arm. Make 'em feel like a million bucks, even if it was just you and not a mansion in the Hills."

"Oh! You're sweet, Billy. If only I could find a sweet boy like you, but my fella, he's a real jealous type, and even if he doesn't want me, he wouldn't tolerate anyone else having me either"—she bites her lip, leaving a stain of lipstick on her teeth—"he's a bad man, Billy, who's killed plenty of men for a lot less. No, as long as he's alive, I'll be alone."

She takes my hands again and grips them in her own, resting her face there while her shoulders shake. "What wouldn't I do to stay here in Vegas with a nice boy like you, Billy?"

My head swims with the possibility. I lean over and breathe in the scent of her: Prell and menthol, with notes of perfume hidden beneath. Her mouth meets mine, and she kisses me until I taste the wax of her lipstick. Her hands guide mine to the buttons on her dress, but it isn't buttons I feel under my fingers when the bell on the door chimes again.

"Oh for...!" a deep voice calls before the door jingles shut again.

She pulls away like there is a fire between us and pushes me back across the Formica counter. "Billy! What have we done! He'll kill us both when he hears, my fella. He has eyes everywhere in this town!"

"It would be worth it, for another kiss like that, and the rest of it." I take a fresh napkin from the dispenser and dab at her tear streaks.

"I feel the same, Billy." She kisses my palm, taking the napkin and dipping it in her water glass. "I felt the same on Monday when I came in here and saw you working back there. I thought, *Why, that is the sort of boy who would treat me right.* If only something would happen to my fella, we could be together, Billy. Together."

She's wiped half of her makeup off and has never looked prettier. I hand her the counter rag to finish the job. "There are a lot of muggings and such, down here after dark. Lots of fellas getting killed, and their secretaries. You are good with a knife, Billy. I saw that on Monday when you made me that first sandwich, cutting up those weenies so thin. I saw how much you liked me. You do like me don't you, honey?"

Water drips down her neck and between those buttons on her dress, my handprint is there, too, still wet from when we kissed. Sticks and Straw Billy would have excused himself to the storeroom, but me, well, I lean over and kiss her again and don't pull away until she bites my lip, not as hard as Penny Gilbert, but in a way that says she likes it.

"I like you," I tell her as she lights another cigarette. "And I'd do just about anything to make you happy, make it so you won't cry like that again. But I'm not so good with a knife as I am with a gun. I can shoot the eye out of a bighorn sheep." I take the cigarette out of her hand and fill my lungs with menthol.

56

She smiles as I cough out the smoke, straightens her dress, and, with a satisfied wink, takes a bite of her sandwich.

Historical Note: On June 20, 1947, Bugsy Siegel—the American mobster largely responsible for the development of the Las Vegas Strip—was murdered at the Beverly Hills mansion of his girlfriend, Virginia Hill. She had taken an unscheduled trip to Paris days earlier. Siegel was first shot across the bridge of his nose, losing his left eye. The gunman was never caught.

––––––––––

Sally Bays is a liberal crunchy trad wife who lives in northwest Washington with her delightful family. She has an MFA from Eastern Kentucky University and can often be found offering workshops at local conventions and events. She recently completed a residency at Hypatia in the Woods. When not writing, Sally dabbles in the homesteading arts for "research."

The Last Frontier

Deborah Grochau

November 13, 2007

GRANDMA IS SMALL AND FRAIL in a baby-blue hospital gown. Her skin is almost as pale as the white pillows propping her up in bed. Grace Kelly's face peers out from the back cover of the biography splayed open on the cream-colored blanket. My grandmother's eyes are softly closed as I pad through the door, trying not to disturb her nap. Too late—her eyelids flutter open, and she greets me. "Hello, Michael."

"How are you feeling?"

"Better. " Her voice is still raspy from the anesthesia. "What day is it?"

"Saturday." I pour water from a pink pitcher into a plastic tumbler and hand it to her.

She sips the water through a paper straw. "I seem to have lost track of time since my surgery." Her voice is stronger now.

"That's understandable." I bend down to kiss her cheek. "Your heart bypass was less than forty-eight hours ago."

"Turn on the news. I want to see what's been happening in the world while I've been lollygagging in the hospital."

I sit on a chair next to the bed and use the remote to flip through channels.

"Stop." Grandma points at the TV. "Are they showing footage of that high rise that was scheduled to explode early this morning?"

"I think they call it imploding."

"Don't correct your elders." She gives me the evil eye, then giggles when I cower like an eight-year-old. "Just tell me which casino they're imploding."

I read the closed-captioning scrolling across the bottom of the screen as clouds of dust float skyward and a building collapses into itself. "The New Frontier Hotel Casino in Las Vegas imploded at 2:37 a.m."

"It was called the Last Frontier when I was there in 1952."

I mute the television and stare at my grandmother. "You don't drink or gamble. What were you doing in Las Vegas in the fifties?"

My grandma's smile is mysterious. "My first and last dirty weekend."

"With Grandpa?"

"No, I didn't meet your grandfather until after I graduated from medical school. He's never heard this story, and I'd appreciate it if you didn't tell him."

I nod and pull my chair close to the side of the bed that isn't blocked by the IV and heart monitor.

She reaches for my hand. "I was a freshman at Scripps in 1952. Before that, I attended an all-girls Catholic school. I was naive and had zero experience with men until I met Tom. He was as irresistible as Marlon Brando in *A Streetcar Named Desire.*"

"You couldn't resist Stanley Kowalski?"

"I know, I was young and stupid." Grandma shakes her head. "Please don't judge me too harshly."

"Grandma, now I'm really intrigued."

Fireworks explode across the television screen as the network replays the pyrotechnical display that took place before the casino demolition. We watch the Frontier Hotel implode again and again.

"Turn off the TV and I'll tell you my whole embarrassing story if you promise not to interrupt me."

I promise and click off the television.

Grandma takes another sip of water and begins. "Tom was a senior at UCLA, ten years older than me and attending college on the G.I. Bill. He told me he loved me, and I believed him. In retrospect, I think he was just looking for an unsophisticated girl to cook and clean for him. He wanted me to drop out of college to marry him, and I almost did. That's why we drove to Las Vegas for the weekend. If we hadn't decided to attend the dinner show at the Last Frontier, I might have gone through with the wedding."

I open my mouth to ask a question, then shut it again when my grandmother releases my hand and puts her finger to her lips. A promise is a promise.

Grandma's voice quivers. "Never mistake control for love. Tom planned the whole weekend. He wanted to see his favorite comedian, Dave Barry, who was playing at the Ramona Room. Josephine Baker was the headliner. He knew nothing about her. Female singers didn't interest him. As far as he was concerned, women were to be seen and not heard."

I frown.

She grips my hand again and laughs. "I was such a meek little mouse back then. Tom picked me up after classes on a Friday afternoon in late April. It took us four hours to get from the Scripps campus to Las Vegas. Back then, the Last Frontier Hotel was in the middle of a Western-themed village. We checked our luggage at the front desk because I was a goody-two-shoes and didn't want to sign the hotel register until we were officially man and wife. Then we wandered around the Silver Slipper Casino, waiting for the eight-thirty show to start. I was still a virgin, so I was both nervous and excited."

My hands are sweating. I really don't want to hear the details of my grandmother's sex life.

Grandma releases my sweaty hand. She dries her hand on the sheet while I rub mine on my pant leg.

"Your face is bright red. I didn't mean to shock you, so I'll try to keep my narrative G-rated. You're an adult now, the

61

same age I was in 1952. It wasn't really a dirty weekend because the wedding night didn't actually happen."

I stand and walk over to the window and watch the sun set on all my childish illusions while my grandmother continues her story.

***

April 25, 1952

Tom's plan was for us to get married in the Little Church of the West after Dave Barry's show. But life doesn't always go to plan. The Last Frontier Village looked like a set from a Hollywood Western except for the Ramona Room, which was the most elegant restaurant I'd ever seen in all my eighteen years. Tom wasn't impressed. He complained when they seated us in the back. We could see empty tables at the front of the room, but the maître d' told us those tables were reserved for Josephine Baker's personal guests. I was embarrassed when Tom made a fuss because I could see the stage just fine from my seat. Tom pouted until the cocktail waitress brought him a beer. I was still underage, so I drank the milk that was included in the Gay Nineties Special he ordered for me. It cost $4.75 and also included an appetizer and an entrée.

The first course was Shrimp Cocktail Deluxe. I wondered where they found shrimp in the middle of the desert. When my prime rib arrived, it was well-done. You know, I prefer my meat rare, but Tom didn't bother to ask my preference when he placed the order. As I lifted my fork to my mouth, I heard a commotion behind me. An elegant Black woman in a feathered headdress, who I assumed was the headliner, led a mixed group of Negroes and Caucasians between the tables to the front of the room.

Tom opened his food-filled mouth. "They're giving the best tables to a bunch of—" Thankfully, his words were muffled by mashed potatoes.

I looked around the room and saw a sea of White faces, except for the few Negroes seating themselves at the closest tables to the stage.

"When did they integrate Las Vegas?" Tom's voice was loud, and other people around us nodded their assent. "I sure hope they're not letting them sleep in the same hotel as us."

Our waiters were very attentive, but they ignored the newcomers. As soon as we finished our main course, our plates were whisked away and they brought us dessert. I noticed the people at the integrated tables didn't even have beverages yet.

The Black woman in the feathered headdress we'd seen earlier came on stage and introduced herself as Josephine Baker. She positioned her chair in the center and sat. Everyone in the room stopped talking and stared. The orchestra started playing, but she didn't get up from her chair. The conductor looked at her, and she motioned for him to stop playing. I'd never seen a Black woman or any woman silence a White man in front of a crowd. I was impressed. Tom was not.

"I didn't pay good money to watch a Black wench sit in a chair. She can go sit with her Colored friends and bring the comedian on." Tom motioned to the waiter to bring him another beer.

"Shush," I said, "she's talking."

"Now, I'm not going to entertain," Josephine said. "You just stay where you are until something happens. I'm going to sit right here till they make up their minds what they want to do."

Three waiters bustled to the front tables and set shrimp cocktails in front of the Colored patrons.

Josephine Baker snapped her fingers. "Now pour them each a glass of champagne."

A sommelier strolled forward with a bottle bathed in an ice bucket.

The singer stood and walked toward the microphone. "That's better. Now, I know y'all came here to hear me sing some jazz, and I'm gonna do that after Dave Barry's set, but first I'd like to sing a French song made famous in the movie *Casablanca*. It's called 'La Marseillaise.'" She pointed to the conductor, who raised his baton.

The room was silent except for Tom, who groused, "She better sing it in English."

The orchestra played the first chord, and I was back in the movie theater with Humphrey Bogart and Paul Henreid. Josephine Baker sang the words in French, but no one joined in the way they had in the 1942 film. I just sat there like Ingrid Bergman with tears welling up in my eyes. We'd seen the movie in my high school French class. Back then, I'd thought it was so romantic when Bogart's character sacrificed his own happiness so that Victor and Ilsa could escape. Now I wondered why neither man asked Ingrid Bergman's character what she wanted. They just made decisions for her. The way Tom made decisions for me.

The song ended, and the crowd applauded enthusiastically. Except Tom. Josephine Baker blew kisses as she exited the stage.

Dave Barry came on, and Tom stood up and cheered. I pulled on his sleeve until he sat down again.

The comedian must have been funny because I could hear laughter all around me, but I couldn't concentrate on his jokes. I kept thinking about Tom's rude remarks. Did I want him making decisions for me? Was I willing to exchange my dream of being the first female in my family to graduate from college in order to be Tom's wife?

Tom was standing and cheering again, and I realized Dave Barry's set was over. "Wasn't he great!"

I nodded.

"Get your coat; we're leaving."

I stayed seated. "But the show isn't over."

"It is for us. I'm not listening to some jungle bunny sing French jazz."

"Her name is Josephine Baker, and according to the program she's an international singing star."

Tom pulled on my arm. "Don't make a scene."

"I'm staying."

"Baby," he cooed, "the sooner we leave, the sooner we can get married."

"Maybe we should wait." The orchestra returned to the stage and started tuning their instruments. Waiters hovered around taking drink orders before the next set.

"Wait for what?" Tom raised his voice, and the men around us turned to stare at him. Their wives looked at their hands folded neatly in their laps.

"Lower your voice."

"Wives don't tell their husbands what to do."

Josephine Baker came on stage and started singing "All Alone." Her presence gave me the courage to whisper, "I'd rather be alone than be married to you."

Tom dropped my arm and stomped away. Josephine's voice washed over me. She sang of "Blue Skies," and my heart lifted. I could be brave like her. I wasn't going to let a bigoted man define me. I was going to earn my degree and be somebody.

***

November 13, 2007

Grandma starts humming "J'ai Deux Amours."

I walk back to Grandma's bedside. "Your date just left you alone in the club?"

"Uh-huh. He missed a great show."

"You were eighteen. Weren't you afraid to be all alone in Las Vegas?"

Grandma reaches for the biography of Grace Kelly she's left face down on the bed, straightens the bookmark, and closes it. "Girls in the fifties were trained by their mothers to carry extra cash in case their dates got fresh, so I was prepared. Luckily, the maître d' made sure Tom settled the bill before he left the restaurant. The cocktail waitress came over to check on me after the show. She told me Tom hovered outside the swinging door to the Ramona Room for fifteen minutes, waiting for me to change my mind and go after him. He left when Black members of the kitchen staff crowded through the doorway and blocked his view. I wasn't alone."

"How did you get home?"

"I picked up my luggage at the front desk, then asked the concierge to call a cab to take me to the bus station. I took the Greyhound to Los Angeles, where one of my roommates picked me up."

"Any regrets?"

"No. Seeing Josephine Baker integrate a Las Vegas casino, if only for one night, gave me the courage to pursue my own dreams. My parents sent me to college to find a husband, but I wanted to be a doctor. On Monday morning, I marched into the registrar's office and changed my major from English to pre-med. I only wish I could have thanked Josephine Baker in person for inspiring me."

Grandma closes her eyes and drifts back to sleep. I hum "La Marseillaise" as I tiptoe out of her hospital room.

Deborah Grochau earned a B.A. from Vassar College and an M.A. in history from California State University, Hayward, before embarking on a thirty-year career in education. She traveled extensively in Europe and the United States to research her novel, *I'll Be Seeing You*, which she is currently shopping to agents. Deborah's novel takes place in the 1940s, before the events described in "The Last Frontier." Josephine Baker is the main character in the short story, and she makes a cameo appearance in Deborah's historical novel. Visit Deborah's website at: www.deborahjoangrochau.com.

A Flash in the Pan

Julianne Douglas

March 17, 1953
Las Vegas, Nevada

RITA'S TRAY CLATTERED onto the bar. "Two Atomics and a dry martini."

Stan flipped a pair of cocktail glasses right side up and filled them with ice. He splashed equal parts vodka and brandy into each, along with a swirl of sherry. "They keep drinking at this rate, we're gonna run out of bubbly," he groused, grabbing an unopened bottle and removing the wire cage with a practiced twist. A raucous burst of laughter from a nearby table muted the pop of the cork. He topped off the cocktails with champagne and set them on her tray before they'd stopped fizzing.

Rita leaned over the bar and skewered a couple of olives. "Not much longer," she said, plopping the fruit into the oily gin he was straining into a wide-mouthed glass. "It's already after four."

Stan snorted. "Don't be surprised if they drink right through it. Always do. Now, outta the way. Phyllis, whaddya need?"

Rita tossed some napkins onto the tray. Taking care not to slosh the martini, she eased her way back onto the floor. Why on earth would anyone drink right through it? Hadn't they come expressly to see it? But then again, she conceded, watching a B-list actor strut past with a sequined showgirl on his arm, maybe some of them merely wanted to be *seen* seeing it.

This was, after all, a private—and therefore exclusive—party. According to Phyllis (who'd worked at the Desert Inn since it opened and knew everything there was to know about the place), an invitation to a Sky Room viewing was quite the prize. Every few weeks, the glass-walled, third-floor lounge—one of the highest vantage points in Vegas—would close to the public at three in the morning. Once the tables were wiped and the bar restocked, Walter and Toni Clark would usher their special guests into the sleek interior. The gatherings lasted past dawn.

Rita had only been in Vegas a month. She'd been lucky to snag a job at the Desert Inn, even luckier to land in the Sky Room rather than the casino or the restaurant downstairs. Mrs. Clark had happened to pass the door to the hiring office just as Rita mentioned Seattle. Wouldn't you know, the two of them had grown up blocks apart in Garlic Gulch, nibbling cookies from Borracchini's, gagging on peroxide fumes in Mrs. Ventuto's pink salon chair, and whispering trivial transgressions to Father Caramello in the cramped confessional at Our Lady of Mount Virgin. Overcome with nostalgia, Mrs. Clark had hired Rita on the spot. In a token nod to Father Caramello and his lengthy penances, she'd assigned her to the classy confines of the lounge, where Rita got to wear a demure white blouse and knee-length skirt instead of feathers and fishnet stockings.

Easier on her ass, and much simpler to blend in.

Dodging swaying couples—Ted was teasing a Johnny Ray ballad from the piano this time—she headed for the table in the far corner. The Clarks and three guests sat clustered around it, their faces and shoulders repeated on the plate glass that flanked them on two sides. Beyond it, the night was still dark as a sable stole, though, she imagined, not nearly as warm. She pitied the soldiers crouched in crowded trenches with nothing more than the heat of their breath and the blaze of their anxious thoughts to challenge the cold desert air. Having been in the field all night, most would have traded fear for impatience long before now.

Rita set a napkin before each guest and deposited the drinks, careful to match each with its proper recipient. "Thanks, doll." Mr. Clark tried, and failed, to mask his appraising glance with a jovial smile. "New here?"

"Darling, this is the recent arrival from Seattle I was telling you about," Mrs. Clark said, laying a possessive hand on his arm. "We had a lovely chat in the hiring office. Ruby, isn't it?"

"Rita." Rita hugged the empty tray flat against her middle and flashed a humble smile.

"Rita's brother is one of our brave soldiers out at Camp Desert Rock." Mrs. Clark's gaze shifted toward the window. "Is he on the field tonight?"

"I believe so, ma'am."

"Imagine being practically underneath it!" The breathy blond in the low-cut gown leaned forward and swiped her cocktail off the table. "I bet your whole life flashes before your eyes." She took a long swig.

One of the men chuckled. "Those boys aren't in any danger. Uncle Sam needs them to fight the Russkies."

"These things keep improving, we won't need foot soldiers," the other man drawled, leaning back in his seat and lacing his fingers together atop his paunch. "Our designs are so advanced, the commies won't know what hit 'em."

Rita's fingers tightened on the tray as she searched for a way to engage him. He hadn't ordered a drink. "Are you sure there's nothing I can bring to you, Mr.... ?"

His eyebrows rose a fraction, but he answered readily enough. "Landon. Bob Landon. Only fair, since Toni told us your name, Miss Rita..."

"Moretti," she supplied without a blink. "Rita Moretti."

"And no, Miss Moretti, I'm taking a breather. Don't want to nod off before the fireworks."

"We're good for now, Rita," Mr. Clark said, a slight edge to his voice. Annoyed at being upstaged, she supposed. Phyllis had warned her to play nice if she valued her job. "But be sure to come back when we get closer to go-time."

"Of course, sir." She nodded at Mrs. Clark and backed away.

Bob Landon. She repeated the name a few times. It was probably just an alias, but one he wasn't hesitant to share. His patriotic fervor—as well as his Texan accent—seemed a bit forced. She speculated about his connection to Mr. Clark. Was he passing himself off as retired military? An oil magnate? He didn't seem like the type to be involved in organized crime, but you never knew. Turning her back to the table, she scribbled his name on the last page of her pad.

She visited several more tables, taking orders for gin gimlets and Manhattans and the ever-popular Atomics, but none of the customers roused her suspicions. Casino owners, society wives, Hollywood types. One glamorous gal had actually forked over seventy-five dollars at GeeGee's to have her hair pulled up over a mushroom-shaped wire and sprinkled with glitter. Rita saw more than one person stop to touch the outrageous do. As the room grew more crowded and the partiers more boisterous, she had to lean in close to get her orders correct. Didn't want to mess things up and get herself fired, not with so much at stake.

She was picking up a load of drinks at the bar when she saw him, alone at one of the tables. He sat staring off into space, oblivious to the tumult. Every so often, he would start and jot something onto a paper napkin.

She delivered her drinks and made straight for his table. He had just started scribbling again. "A writer?" she asked from behind his right shoulder.

He twisted around, surprised at being addressed, and laughed. "Far from it. Words are not my thing." She caught a glimpse of equations as he folded the napkin and slipped it into the interior pocket of his jacket.

She circled the table to face him. "Exciting night, huh?"

He nodded. "Always wanted to see this." His blue eyes twinkled like the tiny lights embedded in the dark ceiling to mimic the stars.

"You could get a lot closer out on Railroad Pass or Mount Charleston, you know."

"Sure I could, if I had a car. Since I don't, this seemed like the best bet. Drinks and pretty waitresses an added benefit."

She giggled. "So what would you like? Have you tried an Atomic?"

He screwed up his face. "I hate champagne. Don't suppose you have any coffee?"

Most of the guests were drinking like fish. "Sure, I can get you some. Should I open a tab for you, Mr....?"

"Not unless you want to drink with me."

So he wasn't going to surrender his name. "Unfortunately, my shift doesn't end until seven."

"Too bad." His disappointment sounded genuine. "Have you seen it before?"

A guest at a nearby table, wanting to order, waved for her attention. She pretended not to notice.

"No, this'll be my first time, too. I'm hoping no one asks for a drink during the show."

"Bit of a science geek myself. Flew in from Canton, Ohio, just to see it."

"Let me guess. You're a teacher."

His pleasant face broke into a wide grin. "You got it. High school math. We're on spring break right now. Wish I could have brought some of my students along."

"Wouldn't it scare them?"

He shrugged. "Who better to see it? They'll be living longer than we will in this crazy new world, one would hope."

"Miss?" a woman entreated. "We need drinks over here."

"Coming!" she acknowledged. She winked at the teacher. "Back soon with that coffee."

Phyllis and Lottie were ahead of her in the line at the bar. "Dear Lord, my feet hurt!" Phyllis complained. "Tips have been solid, though." She patted her apron pocket. "People turn generous when they stare death in the face."

Rita widened her eyes. "Aren't we safe, this far away? The Atomic Energy Commission insists there's no danger to civilians!"

"What else are they gonna say?" Phyllis scoffed. "You think they really know? This is all new to them. They have no idea how this will affect us forty years from now."

Lottie laughed, setting her ponytail swinging. "Forty years? This planet's gonna light up like a Roman candle long before then. Hey, Stan, what's taking so long? The natives are getting restless."

Rita chewed her lip. No fireworks on her watch, if she could help it. She was doing all she could to keep the nation one step ahead of its foes.

She gazed out the window, where the darkness only seemed to have deepened. Against it, down the Strip, the neon lights of the Pioneer Club and the Golden Nugget blazed with the cold allure of perpetual promise. Beyond them stretched bare reaches of unrelenting desert, the bleak birthing room of an uncertain future. She glanced at her watch—four forty-five. A little more than a half hour to go, and she'd finally get to see it. She wondered if the experience would live up to the photos.

She fought her way through the wall of guests encircling the piano, arms draped over shoulders as they crooned the melancholy verses of "Does Your Heart Beat For Me?" like doomed passengers on a sinking ship, and plunked a glass of soda water down for Ted, who mouthed his thanks. The table that had ordered drinks decided they wanted peanuts, too, so she had to backtrack to the bar to fetch some. Along the way, someone asked for recommendations on diners for breakfast. When she finally arrived with the teacher's lukewarm coffee, she found his table occupied by a middle-aged businessman and his taffeta-clad wife. The table had been empty when they'd claimed it, they said, and no, they hadn't seen where the man had gone. They would, however, take that coffee before it grew cold.

She handed off the cup and scanned the room, but the teacher was nowhere in sight. She cursed herself for getting distracted. If he'd been who he'd said he was, he never would have left the lounge before the blast. She'd let his blue eyes and boyish grin beguile her. But maybe, just maybe, he'd decided to race the clock and duck into the washroom.

"Gotta pee," she informed Lottie, handing off her tray.

"Hurry or you'll miss it!" Lottie warned. Rita nodded and rushed out onto the landing at the top of the stairs.

Two women had paused to chat mid-flight; a group of men loitered in a haze of cigarette smoke beside a potted palm. She strolled past them over to the window near the men's room door. Was he even in there? She couldn't wait much longer before she'd be missed. The door opened and a stranger emerged, shaking water from his hands. Concocting a story about some keys she'd found, she asked if he'd seen the teacher inside. He assured her there'd been no one else in the washroom but him.

Disappointed but not surprised, Rita checked her watch. Five minutes after five—no time to head down to the staff facilities, and she did have to pee. She slipped into the ladies' lounge, praying no one would report her trespass.

She was at the sink when one of the stall doors swung wide.

"Well, if it isn't Miss Rita Moretti!"

The blond from the Clarks' table sauntered up to the basin and nudged her aside in order to slide her own hands under the running stream. "Though I'd wager I'd have trouble finding a man named Moretti on the field tonight. If I did, I doubt he'd know you were his sister."

Rita managed to keep her composure. She'd never been confronted before, not once. Not here in Vegas, not in Berkeley, not in Los Alamos. This dame was good.

"You certainly wouldn't," she said, reaching for a hand towel. "Moretti's my married name. My husband died a few years back." She wiped her hands and extended the towel to the woman, who turned off the faucet to take it.

"Widowed, and so young! Funny Mrs. Clark didn't mention that, and she seemed to know all about you." She tossed the used towel into the wicker basket on the counter and started digging in her shirred silk purse, her mascaraed gaze never straying from Rita's face.

"I don't like to talk about it." Rita closed the topic with a small, but tragic, sigh. "I really must be getting back to work, ma'am."

The woman laughed. "Oh, do call me Jane. That's what Bob calls me. Or maybe you prefer Betsey? Heidi? Even Olga or Ludmilla will do. Names are such slippery things." She extracted a lipstick, puckered her lips, and gilded them with a fresh coat of red.

"Aren't they?" Rita murmured, heading for the door. "Enjoy the rest of your evening, Jane. I have drinks to serve."

"Bob's real name, for example, is Roger MacIntyre," Jane continued, as if Rita hadn't spoken. "British SIS. He hides his accent well, doesn't he?" Rita paused a second too long before reaching for the handle.

"Thought so." Jane grinned. "You gave yourself away rushing about after Pyotr. He's long gone, by the way."

Rita battled a wave of panic. "I found keys on his table."

"Tsk, tsk. I'd expect a better story from someone like you." Jane smoothed her dress over her rather wide hips. "Learn anything interesting tonight? You were so busy jotting on your pad."

"Just keeping my orders straight."

"'Orders,' hmm? Whose orders do you follow, Miss Moretti?"

Rita retreated a few steps from the door and crossed her arms, checking her watch as she did so. Five-ten. "What can I help you with, Jane? I need to get back to the floor. Don't you?"

"Indeed I do." Jane dropped the lipstick into her open purse and snapped it shut. "But what I need more is a partner. I can date only so many men before it gets noticed. As a waitress, you can chat up hundreds a day."

Rita shrugged. "Then get a job as a waitress."

"Waitresses don't earn much." Jane's eyes narrowed. "We can make it worth your while."

"'We' who?"

"I can't tell you that. But I can put you in contact with someone who can."

Rita jerked her head toward the door. "Get out, before I call security."

"You wouldn't risk your position here."

She was right, of course. "I don't want what you're selling, Jane. Stay out of my way."

"But don't we want the same thing—an end to this madness? Parity alone will keep the world safe."

The security of stalemate: It was becoming a common argument. But Rita was not convinced that either side, even her own, would ever abandon the fight for hegemony.

Jane slunk a bit closer. "Consider it, Rita. Working together, we can prevent the unthinkable from happening."

The washroom door opened on a burst of singing. Mrs. Clark stepped inside and stopped short. "Rita? What are you doing here? This place is reserved for our guests."

Rita nodded contritely. "I heard Miss Jane calling for help. She's not feeling well. I was about to fetch you."

Mrs. Clark hurried over and put a comforting arm around Jane. "Poor dear! Those Atomics are stronger than you think. Can you make it back? Rita, bring some water to our table."

Knowing Jane had no choice but to play along, Rita bolted. She heard Jane laugh as the door closed.

The normally sedate Sky Room had become a roiling furnace of color and noise. As soon as Rita plunged inside, patrons plucked at her arms, demanding drinks. She'd barely made it to the bar to retrieve her tray when Ted teased the opening bars of "Atomic Boogie-Woogie," the original piece that had made him famous.

"The end is near!" he shouted over the music. "Time for one last dance!"

Excited screeches erupted as guests grabbed partners and rushed to the dance floor. Swinging in wide, exuberant arcs, they trod on each other's heels and bumped each other's backs. Hair escaped pins; sweat trickled down collars.

Pounding chords drowned out melody, whipping the crowd into a frenzy.

Clutching her laden tray close, Rita navigated through the sea of flailing arms and hurtling torsos toward the owner's table. Mrs. Clark and Jane had yet to return. The men, deep in conversation, hardly acknowledged her as she unloaded a pitcher of water and five glasses. She contemplated alerting Bob Landon to Jane's wiles but decided against it. Mr. Landon might be tracking Jane himself, or worse yet, playing both sides. Judging it best to protect her own cover, Rita melted back into the crowd. It was almost time, and she wanted to claim a place at the window.

The music reached a frantic crescendo. Flushed and panting, the dancers executed their final twirls and slides. Applause exploded as Ted banged out the final measure. "Two minutes to go! Take your places for the countdown!"

The crowd rushed to the windows that faced north toward the Atomic Proving Ground, seventy miles away. The sun would not rise for half an hour yet, but night was loosening its hold. The stars had dimmed; the saucy glare of neon signs waned, anemic; casinos and houses emerged from the dark depths as blocks of ghostly gray. The distant bluffs wore a streak of pink along the ridgeline. Somewhere out there on that desolate plain, a scaffolded tower loomed five hundred feet above the ground like an immense gallows. The beacon of a peaceful future—or a funeral pyre ready for igniting?

The press of bodies pinned Rita against the window, unable to move.

At the bar, Stan consulted his watch and began the count. "Ten. Nine. Eight. Seven…" The guests joined in, their voices husky with anticipation.

***

Out on the field, the siren sounded; the soldiers shut their eyes and shielded their faces. A sudden flash of unnatural light engulfed them in a pall of white silence. One boy, foolish enough to peek, saw the bones of his hand through his skin. The angry air scorched the soldiers' nostrils and singed their lungs; they held their breath until the ground jolted beneath them and dislodged cries of amazement and terror from their chapped lips. With a deafening crack, the shock wave arrived, assaulting the berms of heavy earth that sheltered them and toppling loose dirt upon their heads. Echoes rumbled like thunder off the surrounding mountains as the men gnawed on their misgivings and waited for the order to advance.

***

Rita sucked in her breath as an unearthly glow flared on the horizon. For a moment, the sky lit up as bright as midday. Far beyond the end of the Strip, an enormous orange cloud stretched toward the heavens, a writhing, churning testimony to man's destructive genius. There was no forcing this billowing genie back into its fractured bottle, no appeasing the scientists' thirst for knowledge nor the politicians' hunger for power. It was one thing to consider such a weapon in the abstract, quite another to observe its prodigious force firsthand. What hubris to think her paltry efforts might somehow contain it.

Stunned into silence, the crowd watched the cloud swell and expand, enormous and forbidding even at this distance. A full minute passed before someone whistled, a long, appreciative note. Tentative claps followed, prompting a surge of cheers. By the time the seismic wave passed through town, rattling windows and shaking floors, the guests were stamping their feet and offering toasts.

"Music!" someone shouted. Ted's spirited "Yankee Doodle" spurred them to sing.

"A round of drinks, on the house!" Mr. Clark declared after several verses left them hoarse. Hoots of gratitude welcomed his offer.

Rita could not pull her gaze from the seething cloud that spread ever wider in the clean light of dawn.

"Miss? Miss?" Someone tapped her shoulder. "Bring us some drinks before the line gets too long!"

Rita turned and stared numbly at the guests' avid faces.

Did they not understand the enormity of what they'd just witnessed?

But perhaps they did. Perhaps they, like everyone in Vegas, in all of America, were coping with this frightful reality the only way they knew how: by dancing and drinking, singing and gambling, shopping and working and playing and loving, skirting the abyss that yawned at their heels.

A draw was not possible; this race would proceed to its unforeseeable end.

They had no choice but to run it, best as they could.

Rita straightened her shoulders and flipped open her pad. "Of course, sir," she said, pencil poised. "What can I get for you?"

Julianne Douglas submitted her first story to *Good Housekeeping Magazine* at the age of twelve. A kind editor there encouraged her to keep writing, and decades later, she's still at it. Julianne earned a Ph.D in French literature from Princeton University and has written two historical novels set in Renaissance France. Her blog, *Writing the Renaissance* (www.writingren.blogspot.com) features articles on sixteenth-century history and culture, reviews of historical novels, author interviews, and musings on the novelist's craft. A longtime member of the Historical Novel Society, Julianne has attended all but two of the North American conferences.

Up and Atom

B. K. Froman

May 5, 1955

"THEY'LL APPRECIATE THE HONESTY." Cal Peters sat spraddle-legged on the vinyl couch, the turpentine scent of fresh paint surrounding him. He massaged his temples, studying the new linoleum tiles covering the floor.

His knees nearly touched the woman perched on the chair across from him. He glanced at her smooth skin. She remained motionless. Her curly brown hair framed her green eyes riveted on his face. She was silent. This morning, a reporter had jokingly nicknamed her Mrs. America. He called her Molly.

"Nobody takes this seriously anymore." The new couch made squelching noises as he slouched back into it. "*The Albuquerque Tribune* says Las Vegas students don't even look up when they hear a detonation. It's old hat. The Vegas Chamber of Commerce mails calendars with our test dates so they can fill hotels. They've built sky bars so tourists can watch our clouds rise from sixty-five miles away. Right now, the Sands Hotel is chewing my butt because Operation Cue is nine days late, like I can control high winds."

He glanced across the room at Mr. America in his upholstered armchair, holding a newspaper as though he was actually reading it. In front of the big window, his three children in various sizes, dressed in their Sunday best, silently played Parcheesi. From the kitchen, the bluesy notes of "In the Still of the Night" drifted from the radio.

"If this goes well, everyone will see that the new Federal Civil Defense Administration uses tax dollars to save lives." Cal clenched and unclenched his fists. "Now people can know the secrets of how to survive an atomic attack. If they don't lose hope, they can live. America can—"

A rap on the doorframe stilled his words.

"Mr. Peters?" A short workman in a dirty denim jacket leaned into the room. He scowled, looking around. "Sorry to bother you so late, sir. I saw lights on here in House Two. Thought I'd make sure there hadn't been any more … problems."

Cal glanced around, wondering how this looked to his construction manager. How long had the man been listening to him talk to a mannequin? Cal cleared his throat. "I'm … planning tomorrow's speech. And all is fine since I fired two of your crew, Don."

"Yes, sir. About my boys—"

"I don't give a ballistic damn why those jackasses undressed two mannequins in House One. What sets my teeth on edge is the risk. If I hadn't personally checked the houses before this morning's press tour, you can bet there would've been photographs in every newspaper across the nation showing two mannequins in bed, copulating.

"Obviously, those two clowns don't care how millions of dollars of donated clothing and furnishings will withstand an atomic blast. So they're fired! Do you think any corporation would donate to this op or any US citizen would support Civil Defense if they thought we treated survival as a joke?"

"No, sir, you're right." In the uneasy pause that followed, Don stared at Mrs. America, then Cal, his glances shuttling between the two, his eyebrows knitting together. Finally, he added, "Me and my wife, we take Doom Town—I mean Survival Town—serious."

"Good. And please remind the crews again to use the official name so the media gets behind it. Survival Town!"

"Of course, sir. I just wanted to say that my wife helps the Las Vegas Women's Civil Defense. She even bought a special dish to serve doughnuts to the reporters up on Nob Hill. It's some kinda fancy Franciscan China Atomic Plate. It's decorated with dots and rays and glazed in lead, so the food will be safe. She thought it would make the bomb blast more special."

"Remember, we're not calling it a bomb. 'Atomic device' carries a more positive message." Cal stood and grabbed his jacket, giving Molly a quick last glance. "Thank your wife for volunteering. I'm confident you've already assured her that at ten miles from ground zero, she and the doughnuts will be quite safe. Speaking of food ..." he continued without giving Don a chance to reply. "If you see Phil Dodds, tell him to confirm the soup cans were buried."

"I'll tell him, but I saw his boys shoveling dirt over cans, bottles, and cartons in trenches. One of his crew put fresh meat, flown in from Chicago, into the fridges. Why—"

"Because we test radiation levels before and after, so people know what's safe to eat after an attack." Cal's voice carried the gruffness of a football coach ending instructions and hustling players onto the field. He squeezed through the doorway, past Don. He wished he could look back at Molly and her family, who would take his confessed worries and self-doubts to the grave with them, but he kept walking. His one remaining thread of patience had sprouted thorns.

Outside, the Nevada night caressed his face with coolness. He paused and closed his eyes, working his jaw loose. The pungent scent of Joshua trees and greasewood bushes calmed his mind. Above, the inky sky with pinpricks of stars stared down. Don joined him, shoving his hands in his jacket pockets. They listened to the transformer substation at the edge of Survival Town, humming electricity through multiple lines on wooden poles. The red light flashed atop the hundred-foot radio tower, proof that communications in Survival Town were working fine.

Don chin-jutted at the line of well-dressed plaster-people anchored at measured distances, facing the blast. "The dummies look ready."

"The Langley company donated fifty fully-haired *mannequins*. If you talk to anyone, be sure to call them mannequins. It's friendlier." Cal huffed a weary sigh. Both men stared into the darkness. From habit, their gazes soon moved back to the radio tower. The pennants hung limp from the guy wires.

"Looks like the wind finally died. We're confirmed to go in the morning, right?" Don said.

Cal nodded.

"My construction guys you fired … I'm gonna need 'em tomorrow. It's too short notice to get anybody else with clearance." Cal didn't answer. Don looked behind him at the living room window, then back at his boss. "You okay? You eaten lately?"

Curses exploded in Cal's head. He shouldn't have become unhinged this morning, but he was an engineer on a mission, not a hand-holder for employees. This test site was only a paycheck to the crews, but it was his chance to get to Washington. Logic and honesty in killing atomic myths was what was needed in the department, not some political hack. He could save more lives if he had more influence—because his FCDA brochures sure weren't drawing anybody's interest.

He exhaled another long breath. Probably, he was already a laughingstock for firing two carpenters for messing with plaster-people, and if it got out that he'd used a mannequin as a counselor, he'd never live it down. "Tell your boys to be in the trenches at four thirty."

"Thanks. They've learned their lesson. I'm sending them to get Atomic Burgers for the crew. You look like you could use one. Maybe an Atomic Shake? It's chocolate with charred marshmallows on top. Real good."

Cal shook his head. "Thanks. I'll hit the mess tent."

"Better skip that muddle. Those five thousand volunteers and military hanging 'round the barracks make everything an eternal wait. I've had to send a crew over there every day, unplugging toilets."

Cal walked away, calling over his shoulder, "Just like a real disaster, huh? All part of the experiment, seeing what it takes to care for thousands of people after an atomic explosion. Make sure the electricians check the time-lapse cameras again. Nothing can go wrong tomorrow. I'm counting on you."

Don waved. "See you at atomic dawn!"

Cal kept walking, grousing, "It's called an atomic flash. Why do people make up words when they don't understand something? No wonder my job is hard."

***

He skipped eating and slept a couple of hours in the Civil Defense trailer. At 3:00 a.m., he drove to Nob Hill. The lights of a long motor caravan snaking through the desert, coming from Las Vegas, met him. At the entry gate, he joined journalists and TV broadcasters, showing their blue military name badges imprinted with a white atomic cloud.

Bundled in a coat and wool hat to ward off the chill, he roamed the craggy hill, glad-handing contacts. Others were guided into bleachers, sitting hip to hip in the dark, waiting. TV crews continually checked their camera feeds. Cal thanked the lady handing out doughnuts. "Your husband said you're using a special plate."

"He wouldn't let me bring it." Her face mushed as if each word rankled her. "Don said it was too expensive to lug around in the rocks. Now, he's gonna sell it as a collector's item."

Cal nodded, but he wasn't listening. He scanned the surroundings, unable to see much in the dark. He knew that two miles from ground zero, fifteen hundred troops waited beside their four-foot-deep slit trenches. The radio reported that forty-five miles away, Mount Charleston, a favorite local viewing point, was clogged with tourists and officials from other cities. Sixty-five miles away, residents had lawn chairs and coolers in the desert, north of "the city that never sleeps." The Dawn Bomb partyers always began drinking at midnight and continued until the flash, or till they passed out.

The activity around Nob Hill energized him. Unconsciously, he clapped his fingertips together. Finally! Taxpayers would look inside tests that were formerly secret. Now they'd take Civil Defense seriously.

At 5:09 a.m., the loudspeaker announced, "Put on your goggles. Observers without goggles must put their arms over their eyes and turn away from the blast." Cal checked the crowd. They were following instructions. He gave a tiny finger clap.

"H minus one minute," the loudspeaker warned. The crowd stilled, staring into the blackness. Cal kneeled, bracing his back against a van.

"H minus ten," the voice called.

"Nine..." the emotionless countdown continued. It seemed everyone was holding their breath.

"Zero."

A blinding flash exploded across the landscape.

Cal's Civil Defense brochures had described it as brighter than a thousand suns. An otherworldly whiteness filled the landscape, up, down, all-around. Several people in the crowd cried out. Cal knew those were the ones without goggles. They'd seen the bones in their arms through their flesh.

Gasps sounded as the thermal wave chased the light. The hot sensation of opening a furnace door had heat-slapped their faces, then quickly subsided.

The voice announced, "The blast wave will arrive in approximately thirty seconds." Some people who'd read Cal's brochure covered their ears. In moments, bodies jerked as though they'd been both shoved and slapped at the same time. The air cracked as a few people fell over. One observer's shoe blew from his left foot.

Journalists tore the goggles from their heads, pointing cameras, trying to capture images of the fireball transforming into a cloud. Orange, red, and purple vapors churned, then unrolled like a huge doughnut. Red and brown streamers spiraled downward as a white parachute-top formed.

"Ohs" and "Ahs" rose from the crowd. The domed top floated higher and higher. "Fabulous!" "Beautiful!" "Terrifying!" All eyes stayed fixed on the white cloud blooming in the dawning sky. Ugly gray and black fungal strands twisted and churned beneath it.

After fifteen minutes, the loudspeaker announced, "An ice cap has formed on the top of the cloud at thirty-five thousand feet." It rose no higher.

Within minutes, troops climbed from their slit trenches. Fuzzy shapes of tanks tracked across the desert, then disappeared, along with the men, into the dust, fog, and smoke on the ground.

In less than an hour, the loudspeaker reported, "Military exercises have been successful. We've confirmed the ability of American troops to complete objectives during an atomic event. You are invited to the post-op presentation at ten hundred hours in the community tent."

By now, the sky was brightening. The cloud had lost its stem and dirty colors. It looked like any other cloud in a blue sky. The top began to flatten as the wind, like a gentle hand, pushed it toward Utah.

Layers of dust and smoke still obscured ground zero. Some reporters feverishly clacked typewriters balanced on their laps. Others scribbled in notebooks. TV journalists from the UK lined up military authorities for interviews and assurances that the grit and dirt of fallout had lost its radiation. It would be twenty-four hours before anyone would be allowed to enter Survival Town.

Cal smiled as he climbed into the FCDA van. He was due for a nap before the post-event talk. Everything had gone perfectly.

***

At the post-op, he reminded everyone that sixty-five experiments had been conducted in Survival Town during Operation Cue. "They're listed on the Federal Civil Defense Administration—FCDA—brochures you were given. Contact us for results of those tests.

"Also, in everyone's packet, including reporters and volunteers, you'll find your personal assignment in the blast area tomorrow. Some will work with the fire units, others in food service, and others in the medical corps. Each of you will have an opportunity to inspect the buildings."

He held up a brochure. "The FCDA thanks you for reminding Americans..." He deepened his voice, bullying it into the microphone. "Preparedness leads to survival! Survival leads to ultimate victory over the Soviet aggressor!"

During the applause, Cal handed the microphone to the technical boys for further Q&A. Excitement pulsed through his thoughts, making his hands tremble. *Today will hallmark America's readiness for the atomic age.*

***

Two days later, his secretary, Irene, laid the first newspaper articles on his desk. They were highly favorable, mainly from scientists and physicists commending the research. Patriotic citizens in Las Vegas and across the country added testimonies they were proud to have donated to the experiment.

However, by the end of the week, the headlines were much different.

"Hell at Yucca Flats"

"The 6-Million Dollar Atomic Circus"

"A Look into the Bowels of Hell"

"Dust Piles Over Dead in Doom Town"

"Televisions Go Dark as Mushroom Cloud Crosses into Utah"

"Pasadena—300 Miles West—Felt the Earth Shake"

"Americans Split Over Use of Atomic Weapons"

Despite Cal's repeated corrections, the media had labeled the story location as Doom Town, Nevada.

Article after article depicted scenes of carnage and a town ripped apart. Reporters had found the broken bodies of mannequin-residents lying in the desert unsettling. The medical corps did a fine job of gathering the bits and bodies, wrapping them in blankets, and carrying them on stretchers to ambulances like actual victims, but the images of holes in heads or ripped-away arms or burnt torsos made fearsome photos.

The *Las Vegas Review-Journal* described "complete domestic collapse" with "sands shifting through wrecked doors and shards of shattered glass everywhere."

"What about the successful news?" Cal hurled the newspapers against the wall.

Irene flinched.

"Power was restored in hours," he ranted, "even though two poles snapped. The radio station was transmitting by the next day. House One collapsed without crushing the mannequins in our basement shelter. Proof that we know how to keep buildings from killing people. House Number Two didn't even fall in." He briefly thought of Molly, then pushed her out of his mind.

Irene scowled, her words coming at him low and sharp. "Newspapers said the radiation levels in House Two were so high, no one could get inside for thirty hours. When rescuers finally entered, it looked like a hurricane had turned glass into splinters and doorknobs into shrapnel. Anyone can go see those poor mannequins at the Penney's store in Vegas."

She picked the papers off the floor, smacking them onto his desk. "They're displayed along with before and after pictures. It's sickening."

"Calm down." Cal waved away her drama. "Penney's generously supplied the clothes and wanted them back after we recorded the results. They thought it would draw customers. We're fine with that."

Irene frowned. "I'm never buying a pair of nylons or synthetic undergarment again. I don't want to be fried like a chicken." She turned to leave.

"A thick coat and hat would be a better investment," Cal muttered. "Preferably lead-lined."

She whirled around. "You think this is funny? Why even test clothing? It's not like anybody will have time to change dresses when the warning sounds—*if* there is a warning. Look at those pictures. One article says nuns on Mount Charleston started praying when the bomb went off."

"Stop!" Cal knuckle-rapped his desk. "You *know* Civil Defense is about anticipating war. *Not* fighting it. If you don't get it, then how am I going to make John Q. Public understand?"

She froze, her hand on the doorknob, staring at him. The distant sound of bulldozers clearing away Doom Town for the next op hummed through the windows. One detonation every three weeks was scheduled.

He exhaled. He shouldn't have yelled, but he wasn't going to apologize. Unfortunately, silence prickled his nerves. He never knew what to say into the gap.

Irene's words cut the stillness. "That film of the school bus suddenly turning black and the tires melting? I thought of my children inside that bus, coming home from school. And the cars weren't any safer." Her voice rose, "Good grief! We mail brochures promoting the automobile as the 'all new multipurpose survival tool, sheltering or transporting people during an attack.'"

"Yes, we need to edit the—"

"Those cars looked like burn barrels! The buildings were nightmares. Girders were twisted, metal sheds folded over—"

Cal's hand flew up, signaling her to halt. "We knew many of the structures in the one-mile radius would collapse. It's better to find the vulnerable points now and redesign buildings *before* rather than *after* an attack."

"But worst of all," she continued, "besides 'dead' plaster families lying around … the nightmare that keeps playing in everybody's mind is the time-lapse footage. "One of those houses looked *exactly* like my grandma's home. Most folks around here live in those single-story ranch houses.

"In that slow-motion footage, the paint boils off our siding, then flames shoot like geysers up our walls. But don't worry, a hundred-and-sixty-mile-an-hour wind blows the fire out. Then, surprise! The blow reverses, sucking dirt and rocks back into the cloud and ripping every board and shingle away until the ground is bare. All of us are thinking, *That could be me, poisoned and blown apart.* And it all happened in two-point-three seconds.

"You gave everyone a front-row seat, watching bombs explode that were twice the size of what we used in Japan." Tears gleamed in her eyes.

He squinted. "You thought you were safe because we won the war? Had you never considered atomic weapons could be turned around and used on us? This is the new era. This is why we're preparing."

She shook her head. "The papers are calling it a 'homegrown Hiroshima.' It dropped right into our living rooms. No wonder people are protesting in—"

"Enough!" Cal shouted, his fists clenching and unclenching. The phone rang.

He ignored it. "Overreaction is typical to anything new, but this can help us. We *want* people to be afraid. We *need* families to quickly build shelters and spend Sunday afternoons practicing drills. If the public sits around like those brainless mannequins, they'll end up like them. Our innocence has passed.

"The moment we split the atom, no one could put that bullet back in the barrel. Our job now is to mitigate an atomic future. Operation Tot-Tag will launch next in Vegas. Children will wear steel necklaces so they'll be easier to identify in case of injury or death. *Duck and Cover* films will saturate schools, and we'll give classrooms lead curtains to cover the windows."

She glared at him with stinging silence. The phone jangled two more times. Finally, she whispered, "You don't get it.

You're so busy trying to save lives, you can't see how you're damaging them. It needs to change."

"Go to your desk and answer that phone, please." He looked away until she'd left.

He should fire her, but she was a whiz at filling out requisitions. Besides, only she knew where everything was filed. Why couldn't all secretaries be like Molly and just listen when a man was stressed?

"It's the federal office in Washington." She snapped each word.

"I've got a meeting." He walked from his office, past her. "Tell Herb I'll phone back as soon as I'm done." Feeling her eyes hatchet his back, he stepped outside the trailer. Circling the nearby Joshua tree, he scrubbed his fingers through his hair and kicked rocks. The operation had gone perfectly. This much pushback was unexpected. He'd truly thought people would say, "Wow! Now I see why this is important. Thanks for the truth. I respect that."

Instead, folks were crying over mannequins. They shouldn't have been surprised. He'd forewarned reporters that Survival Town was built to be destroyed. Why didn't the press focus on victories like the fact that the propane and gas tanks didn't explode? The reinforced buildings didn't crumble. Services, including phones, functioned in forty-eight hours. Everything was not lost.

He'd advocated to give people facts. Let them have an honest look at how their taxes were being spent. Now, it felt like a thankless job to show people the truth.

A flatbed truck passed, ballooning dust as it headed for Vegas. Two Buicks, burnt like fire logs, were strapped to the bed. The dealership wanted them back for a patriotic display.

He scanned the horizon toward the city. *How had Las Vegas succeeded?* In some mystical way, the city kept weathering time and cultural clashes, even in its early days when gambling had been banned. Later, when only snakes and roadrunners scooted through the greasewood bushes, Vegas had billed itself as the Gateway to Hoover Dam and become a tourist destination. Surely its reputation should've tanked when it became Sin City, but the city embraced it and grew. Now, they'd repackaged themselves as Atomic City. They thrived. Those were his kind of people. Ever-changing. If only other places were like Vegas, full of people that understood how to adapt to survive.

Irene stuck her head out the trailer door. "Mr. Peters! Washington phoned back. They said to get you out of whatever meeting you're in."

Her voice sounded lighter. *Maybe even smug?* He didn't move.

"As you like to say, 'up and at 'em,'" she called out. "The higher-ups are waiting, sir, and you know that going from survival to destruction only takes two point three seconds." She closed the door.

Her words deflated him. Cal slow-walked to the trailer, his mind churning. Even though thirty-five million TV viewers had watched Operation Cue, he predicted all future ops would be closed to the public's eyes—and he wouldn't be going to Washington.

He believed in honesty, but if people yowled about plaster dummies, how would they react to the next experiments, testing cures for radiation sickness on live pigs? Or the upcoming op with a monkey in an auto-piloted plane? The animal would be sent into the radioactive cloud, testing what would happen if a fighter pilot had to fly through those vapors.

Disheartened, he cursed himself. It was a two-edged sword, honesty. You could end up getting more than you wanted: fear instead of trust. He was a fool for believing people were strong enough to stomach the truth. Like castor oil, they could only swallow it in small doses.

His fists clenched. There was a schedule to keep and new data to gather. Already, they knew more about radioactivity than infantile paralysis or the common cold. New experiments needed to be done behind closed gates. America must survive this Cold War.

That was the mission.

With a longing look toward the ever-changing city of Las Vegas, he took a deep breath, then went inside.

B.K. Froman is an award-winning writer, radio/TV talent, and university educator who creates stories about dealing with the changes life throws at us. Author of nine novels, her works have been recognized by Women Writing the West, LAURA Short Fiction and WILLA Novel Awards, Arizona Writers Association, Oklahoma Book Awards, Will Rogers Medallions, and Barnes and Noble Top 20 Indie Novel. B.K. enjoys using wry humor and clever dialogue to remind her readers that we may repeat history, but life is all about change. For more information, go to www.barbarakayfroman.com

Millie & Loretta at the Desert Oasis

Ana Brazil

Autumn 1959

MILLIE LINGERED OUTSIDE the Lucky Ladies Café, just steps away from a man playing the penny slots. She had only enough money for a cup of coffee, but the aroma of today's Breakfast of the Day, the 99-cent Gambler's Special, enticed her. Still, who in the world could eat an eight-ounce New York steak, two eggs, potatoes, toast, and orange juice at nine o'clock on a Sunday morning?

"Your husband," a woman spoke from behind Millie's back, "is he as big a bastard as mine?"

The question couldn't possibly be for Millie; this was her first visit to Las Vegas, and she didn't know anyone. Still, at the combination of *husband* and *bastard*, she was all ears. *What kind of woman talks about her husband like that in public?*

Maybe, Millie twinged as her stomach groaned, *this is my big chance. I've been here for two days and this is the first time I've been out of Floyd's sight. Checkout's soon, so it's now or never.*

Millie turned around slowly, surprised to find a lone woman gazing at her. She was dressed in a stunning silver-and-black brocade dress with a sweetheart neckline. Her raven-black hair had been teased and curled into an elaborate updo, and her red lips were perfectly painted. Older than Millie, possibly by twenty years, she stood as confidently as a queen, as though she owned the place.

Millie, dressed in a red gingham sleeveless blouse and black pedal pushers and her blond hair stretched tight in a ponytail, almost took a step backward in reverence. "Excuse me. Were you talking to me?"

"Yes, I was." The woman held a porcelain coffee mug in her left hand, and Millie's eyes went straight to the glistening gold and sparkling diamonds on her ring finger.

The woman took a long sip from her mug, as though she were relishing a cocktail instead of coffee. "I wanted to know if your husband was as big a bastard as mine."

Millie had been hoping for a moment like this, hoping to find another woman in the casino who knew how awful marriage was and could help her out. But those rings made her doubt. *Is she getting divorced or not? Maybe she's only wearing her rings until her divorce comes through?*

Suddenly, the nearby slot machine paid off and hundreds of pennies cascaded to the hardwood floor. As the player struggled to capture his winnings with a bucket, Millie wondered, *How can you win if you don't take a chance?*

And then, *If you're going to do it, you better do it now.*

"He is, as a matter of fact." Millie took a deep breath, measuring her next words carefully. "Floyd Alford is the biggest bastard in Los Angeles County, and I came to Las Vegas to divorce him."

***

Loretta finished her Irish coffee in three sips; it was time to introduce herself to Floyd Alford's wife.

"I'm Loretta Conti."

"I'm Millie. Millie Alford," the young woman gulped. "Why would you even think…How did you know….?"

Loretta's eyes creased with concern. *I know a defeated woman when I see one.*

But instead of responding directly, Loretta asked, "Would you like an Irish coffee, Millie?"

"Is that alcohol? I don't—"

"Black coffee, then." Loretta put her hand on Millie's bare arm, turning her away from the café. "We'll have more privacy in the celebrity showroom next door. They don't start rehearsing until this afternoon."

As they walked through the lobby toward the showroom, Millie said, "You know a lot about this place."

"I should," replied Loretta. "My husband owns it."

Millie's gaze passed from a wiry craps dealer talking to a fishnet-stockinged cocktail waitress and then to a uniformed security guard patrolling the casino. "Your husband owns this place?"

"With a few friends," Loretta responded lightly. "But Carmine manages it."

Before Loretta led Millie through the thick curtains and into the softly lit lounge, she motioned to the cocktail waitress to bring her another Irish coffee, heavy on the whiskey. For Millie, Loretta ordered a maple-frosted doughnut and a carafe of black coffee. As Loretta knew from experience, this conversation might take a while.

Once they were settled across from each other in the showroom, Millie asked, "But how *did* you know that I was married to a..."

Although Millie had said *bastard* easily enough a few minutes ago, she seemed incapable of repeating it now. Loretta—who'd been brought up with profanity and prayers in equal measure—had no such problem.

"*Bastardo,*" Loretta spat out the word in Italian, just like she had yelled it at Carmine earlier this morning.

Millie looked away from Loretta and toward the entrance, as though she was expecting to see her bastard husband coming after her. Instead, the waitress entered and placed their mugs and doughnut on their table. She was about to pour the coffee, but Loretta thanked her and took over the task.

"I know it's not a very popular idea." Loretta addressed the carafe of coffee before looking at Millie, "But women have to

97

help each other out, especially when bastards are involved, don't you think?"

"I—I don't know," replied the younger woman. "The girls I know in Los Angeles are too busy taking care of their husbands to help other girls. Although," Millie crossed her fingers in her lap for luck, "one of the other operators at the office told me that she heard a girl could get a divorce in Nevada. She called it a no-fault divorce?"

After pronouncing *no-fault* as though it were a foreign language, Millie tore off a piece of doughnut and dunked it in her coffee. Once again, she glanced toward the entrance to the showroom.

"Don't worry," said Loretta, who also made sure to know where her husband was at all times, "I've got my eye on the entrance. I'll let you know if anyone looks in."

As Millie dunked another doughnut chunk, Loretta got down to business.

"Getting a divorce comes down to money. You have attorney's fees and court fees. You have to live in Vegas for six weeks; sometimes more. Rich women stay in the hotels; some even rent entire houses. Other women stay at the ranches outside of town. The women on tight budgets rent rooms in homes."

Loretta asked as kindly as she could, "Do you have any money?"

"A little." Millie smiled, obviously proud of her answer. "I type papers for other students on Friday nights when Floyd's at his weekly poker game. He doesn't know I do it. But it's not even forty dollars yet." After pausing for a few seconds Millie asked, "I'm going to need more than that, aren't I?"

Closer to six hundred dollars, Loretta held back from telling Millie. But Loretta was here to help, so she gave Millie the good news. "Many women take jobs while they're here. Cocktail waitresses and cigarette girls can make good money."

"I've been working since high school," replied Millie. "I waitressed a little but never worked in a club. I'm a telephone operator, and right now I make just enough to pay Floyd's tuition and our housing and meals.

"It wasn't always this way," Millie almost seemed to apologize to Loretta. "When Floyd and I were in high school, he said he'd take care of me. All I had to do was work and get him through college, and after he graduated, he'd get a big job. Then he'd buy a four-bedroom house, and we would have children."

Millie's eyes watered, and Loretta waited for tears to follow. But Millie seemed a little stronger than the other women Loretta had counseled through the years and wiped away her own tears.

"Floyd wants two boys." Millie blew her nose into her napkin. "But he couldn't get a job after college, and instead he's going to law school."

Once more, Loretta caught Millie looking at her gold-and-diamond engagement and wedding rings.

"Do you have children, Mrs. Conti?" asked Millie. "Is that why you're still with your husband?"

"Yes, I have children. Two boys, both in college. And yes, I'm still with my husband because of family."

"But if your children are in college—"

"It's not my children that keep me here; it's the rest of my family. I've got family all over Vegas, and they would never let me leave Carmine."

"Maybe…maybe you could go to Reno?"

Mamma mia! Did Millie know nothing about Italian families?

"I've got family in Reno. Carson City also. They'd know right away if I ever tried to get a divorce. As I said, they'd never let me leave Carmine."

Millie seemed to realize she'd hit a brick wall with Loretta. "If I can get the money together, and get a room and job, how do I find a lawyer?"

Just as Loretta asked Millie if she had a pencil and paper, the curtains into the showroom entrance were pulled apart and Loretta heard a young man call out.

"That's her. That's my wife."

Loretta cursed quietly. She'd let herself get distracted by this blond, spaghetti-thin young woman and hadn't been watching for Carmine. Now, her husband and a man sporting a loud Hawaiian shirt entered the showroom and stood at her table.

"Well, isn't this a pretty picture." Carmine was in his Sunday best, a navy-blue suit with a narrow light-blue tie. He grinned widely, turning on his casino manager charm full blast. "You lose your wife and my wife finds her. What are the odds?"

"I've been looking all over for you." Millie's husband shook a finger at his wife. "I should have put a bell around your neck."

Carmine turned on his wife. "You should be ashamed, Loretta. Mr. Alford's been looking for his wife for a half hour."

After twenty-five years of marriage to Carmine, Loretta was rarely ashamed of anything she did, but she also knew how the game of *Make Your Husband Look Strong* was played.

"I was trying to teach Mrs. Alford how to play craps," she replied, "but I wasn't very good at it."

Carmine displayed the smile that made him the Las Vegas Casino Manager of the Year. "That's because craps isn't a ladies' game; she's better off at the slots. But craps is your game, isn't it, Mr. Alford?"

"I like to think so," Floyd replied with a grin.

"Let me make my wife's bad behavior up to you, Mr. Alford." Carmine pulled a handful of chips from his pocket. He motioned for Floyd to open his hand, and Carmine dropped ten chips into his palm.

"I can't play in my own casino," Carmine winked at Floyd, "but why don't we go to the craps table and you can show your wife how it's really played."

***

Millie followed the men and Loretta out of the darkened showroom, needing a few seconds to adjust her eyes to the lobby's strong lights. She pressed her sharp fingernails deep into the palm of her right hand, concentrating on hurting herself instead of giving in to tears in front of Floyd.

Carmine and Floyd walked side by side onto the carpeted casino floor; Millie and Loretta walked together a few steps behind them.

Carmine asked Floyd, "Where did you say you were from?"

"Los Angeles," Floyd responded loudly. "I won a contest. The prize was a weekend anywhere in Las Vegas, and I chose the Desert Oasis."

"You won the Chamber of Commerce's *What's Nifty about Nevada* contest?"

"Sure did, and I've really enjoyed your hospitality, Mr. Conti. It's a shame that I have to return home in a few hours, but I've got classes tomorrow." When Carmine didn't ask which classes, Floyd told him, "I'm in law school at UCLA. I'm going into corporate law once I get my degree."

*Law school...*Millie pressed the nails of her left hand into her palm, trying to dull her never-ending frustration. *Three more years of answering phones to support Floyd.*

The women passed a quartet of men playing at a bank of noisy slot machines, and knowing Floyd couldn't hear her, Millie said, "*I* won that contest. *I* cut out the entry form from the newspaper, and *I* mailed it in. Floyd didn't even know about it until I told him I'd won."

Millie expected some response, appreciation maybe, from Loretta, but the older woman's focus was on her husband, who had led Floyd to an open craps table.

For the first time since Floyd had found her in the showroom, Millie relaxed. She'd stood behind Floyd all weekend as he'd gambled her hard-earned money on craps. He'd ignored her the entire time, which made her certain that once Floyd started playing, he'd continue to ignore her. Which meant that she and Loretta could finish their conversation.

But just as Millie thought she was safe to ask Loretta her most important question—*Does my husband have to know where I live in Las Vegas?* —Floyd called back to his wife.

"Get over here, Millie, and I'll teach you how to play craps."

Soon after telling the craps dealer to *take care of Mr. Alford*, Carmine excused himself with, "Casino business never ends."

He glanced at his wife, and she followed him away from the table, turning around once to mouth to Millie, "I'll be back."

Floyd took his favorite position—to the left of the dealer—and put Millie on his own left, directly opposite the dealer. With Millie as his sole student, Floyd explained everything he knew about craps loudly and with great authority. Millie picked up the rules quickly: The shooter (Floyd) put a chip on the PASS line, selected two dice from the dealer, and threw the dice against the table wall. If the dice came up seven or eleven, Floyd won the amount of his bet and rolled again. If the dice came up two, three, or twelve (craps), Floyd lost. If the dice came up four, five, six, eight, nine, or ten, that number became Floyd's *point*.

Just when Millie thought Floyd had worn himself out explaining, he said, "If I roll that point before I roll a seven, I win even money; if I roll a seven before my point, I lose."

Even though Floyd blew on his dice before throwing them—*for luck*, he explained—he rolled a three. And then a two. He doubled his bet and rolled a twelve. He doubled again and rolled another twelve. He looked at the remaining two chips in his rack and added them to the PASS line. He threw a three.

Millie tilted away from Floyd. He'd lost all his money, and she could sense his simmering irritation. He dug into his pocket, came out with a ten-dollar bill—*groceries for next week*—and cashed it in for more chips. Millie—who'd worked overtime to earn those ten dollars—dug her left thumbnail into her index finger as she watched Floyd bet and lose all of his new chips.

For the first time since he began playing, Floyd looked at Millie instead of the table or his chips. "Don't be such a sourpuss. I'll win it back." Then he studied her. "You're a mess. Go clean yourself up."

Millie escaped Floyd gladly, but it took her a few turns around the casino to find the sign to the ladies' room. Once outside the room, Loretta snuck up to her side.

"Come with me."

Inside the ladies' room, Loretta set Millie down in a pink boudoir chair and wiped away her dried tears and the snot under her nose. Then Loretta wet her hands and smoothed down the blond strands escaping Millie's ponytail. Finally, Loretta took a tube of lipstick from her pocket and applied it to Millie's pale lips.

"Jungle Red," said Loretta as she handed Millie a blotting tissue. "It's my favorite and it…it looks good on you, too."

Millie only wore lipstick when she could test it at the makeup counter, and she'd never worn a color this rich and bright. As she blotted her lips while looking in the mirror, she realized that the red matched her gingham shirt and even seemed to draw some color to her cheeks. She smiled at herself, and to her sudden surprise, she liked the new woman she saw in the mirror.

Millie wondered if Loretta was going to pull a bottle of fragrance from her pocket next. *Please*, Millie hoped. *Something as sophisticated as you are, Loretta. Something like Topaze or Wind Song.*

Loretta did go back into her pocket, but instead of pulling out perfume, she held casino chips in her hands.

"Carmine's not the only one who knows where the chips are stashed. The cashier's desk is open if you want to trade them for money. It's not much toward a divorce, but it's a start."

The weight of the chips in Millie's hand made her thrill with excitement; maybe even got her heart beating brighter. "Why…why are you so nice to me?"

Loretta, painting a fresh layer of Jungle Red on her own lips, responded quickly. "Another woman was nice to me once, and it helped me through some hard times."

Despite her need to know how to divorce Floyd, Millie suddenly wanted to talk more about *that:* women helping women. But before she could ask Loretta anything, a cleaning lady wheeled her cart into the room and Loretta ushered Millie out.

They stopped in front of the Lucky Ladies Café, almost exactly where they'd met each other earlier. Gazing around, Millie could see every part of the casino: the slot machines and the men playing them; the craps, roulette, and blackjack tables—all covered except for the one Floyd played at; and finally, the cashier's desk Loretta had mentioned.

Millie knew that cashing in her chips was the safe thing to do, but even after Floyd's long-winded instructions, the exciting energy of the craps table called.

Just like earlier this morning, a nearby slot machine paid off. And just like earlier, Millie wondered *How can you win if you don't take a chance?*

One bright penny escaped the player's bucket, rolling down the floor toward Millie. Loretta stopped the penny with her shoe.

"Heads or tails?" she asked.

"Heads I cash in," Millie replied without hesitation. "Tails I play."

The women looked at the penny and then each other. Millie gathered Loretta's arm in hers, and together they walked to the craps table.

***

Millie slowed her step as she and Loretta neared the table. Floyd was still the only player, and his rack had been refreshed with a few fresh chips.

"One more bet and I'll get that new bowling ball I want," Floyd informed the dealer.

"Watch this." He placed all his chips from the rack on the table. "All in."

Floyd admired the table for a few seconds and threw his dice against the wall. Just before they landed, he snapped his fingers. "Six!"

"Seven," called out the dealer, collecting all of Floyd's chips.

"Hell's bells!" Floyd glared at the dealer and then looked around the casino, as if he could find Carmine and get ten more free chips. His eyes lit on the gentlemen's room, and he told Millie, "Be in the lobby in five minutes. We're going home."

As soon as Floyd was out of sight, Millie took up her former place at the table, lodged her chips in the rack, and placed one chip on PASS, just like Floyd had explained to her.

Loretta stood at Millie's left, both of them looking directly at the dealer.

"New shooter," said Loretta, leaving no doubt that Millie was at the table to play.

"Shooter bets ten," the dealer replied to the boss's wife.

"Ten?" Millie looked at the blue chip, surprised to see a number ten on the top. She'd assumed that Loretta had given her what Carmine had given Floyd—one-dollar chips.

"You gave me ten-dollar chips?" Millie whispered to Loretta.

"I sure did." Loretta sounded pretty pleased with herself. "Ten dollars will get nowhere in Vegas, but one hundred can open a door or two."

Was it too late to grab the chip from the table? Too late to head to the cashier for a hundred-dollar bill?

But when the stickman offered Millie five red-and-white dice, she crossed her fingers and picked two. She held the dice for a few seconds, excited—and also a little nervous—that after hours of watching Floyd play this weekend, she finally had her turn.

"Here goes."

She tossed the dice and they hit the far wall of the table, bounced, and stopped.

"Seven," called the dealer. "Winner."

Millie took a big gulp of air, not even realizing she'd been holding her breath. A smile spread across her lips, and she thought of the bold Jungle Red lipstick Loretta had lavished on her. "I won!"

Loretta seemed almost as happy as Millie. "You did!"

Millie collected her dice and rolled again.

"Seven again," said the dealer. "Winner, Winner."

Winner, Winner. Again! Millie tingled from head to toe, her feet tapping on the carpet. *Is this what winning feels like?*

She took up the dice but before she could throw again, a chip dropped on the DON'T PASS line.

Millie turned harshly toward the new player. It was Floyd, once again positioned to the left of the dealer and next to Millie.

"You bought more chips and you're betting against me? You want me to lose?"

"You're going to lose," he growled at her. "This is just beginner's—"

Bruised by Floyd's betrayal, Millie threw the dice before he could finish.

"Seven!" The dealer paid Millie and took Floyd's money. "Lucky lady!"

That's me! Millie shimmied with excitement. *I've won three rolls! I'm lucky!*

Millie's shoulders broadened with confidence. She wanted to taunt Floyd with her triumph, but she sensed that he was heating with rage.

Floyd pressed another chip on DON'T PASS. Millie added two chips to her bet. She rolled a ten and established her point. When she rolled another ten to win, loser Floyd swore another *Hell's bells*.

Floyd dug into his pocket and came up empty.

"No more games," he ordered his wife. "It's time to go. Give me your chips, and I'll cash them in."

Millie half expected Floyd to grab her chips, but instead he slouched against the table, obviously expecting her to obey him. When she didn't, he put his hand out to remove her bet.

"Sir, that's not allowed," said the dealer.

"It's all right. She's my wife."

"Not allowed," the dealer repeated as he looked over Floyd's shoulder.

"That's two hundred and seventy dollars," Loretta spoke softly to Millie. "You'll need double that for an attorney and room and board."

Millie picked up the dice, weighing the itch to keep rolling the dice against the very real possibility of losing all her money.

"This is my last warning. Give me those chips." Floyd leaned forward like he was going to take another swipe at Millie's chips, but when two casino guards approached him, he backed away from the table.

"You can find your own way back to LA," he spat out as he started toward the lobby.

Loretta put her arm around Millie's waist. "If you make this next roll, you'll have enough money to get your divorce. And then you'll be free of the bastard forever."

"If I don't make the roll," Millie asked, "what happens then?"

"You roll again," replied Loretta. "Women like us always roll again, Millie. And eventually, we make our point, no matter how many rolls it takes."

"And women like us," Millie leaned against Loretta, "help each other out."

Forgetting all about Floyd, Millie placed all of her chips on her PASS bet. Just before she hurled the dice down the table she called out, "All in!"

Ana Brazil writes historical fiction about curious, ambitious, and totally bodacious women. Her latest historical mystery, *The Red-Hot Blues Chanteuse,* features smart and sassy vaudevillian Viola Vermillion in 1919 San Francisco. Ana's debut mystery, *Fanny Newcomb & The Irish Channel Ripper*, won the IBPA Gold for Historical Fiction, and her short stories have appeared in numerous crime and historical fiction anthologies. Ana is a founding member of the Paper Lantern Writers and a contributor to PLW's *Crafting Stories from The Past: A How-To Guide for Writing Historical Fiction*. Ana lives with her husband in beautiful Oakland, CA. Meet Ana at www.anabrazil.com.

A Hard-Boiled Day's Night

Kurt Larsen

Grand Prize Winner

Las Vegas, 1964

I POP A PILL, THEN EYE the other one still waiting in my hand. One government-issued, rubber-coated cyanide capsule. Strong enough to kill a fucking elephant. My whole unit had them sewn into our uniforms in case we got captured by the Japs. I don't know why I'd kept it so long. Maybe as a reminder that I was one of the few who made it out, survived that hellhole. Or maybe just because I wanted to save it for later. When the time was right.

"Care for another drink?" a cocktail waitress asks, approaching me. She's probably in her fifties, sporting a midriff, her saggy boobs nearly falling out. Thank God they keep the lights dim in here.

"Sure. But no ice this time," I say, slipping the pill into my coat pocket. It finds company with a few more of its friends down there—uppers and downers, but mostly pain pills. I like the adrenaline rush of not knowing which one I'll grab.

I'd just pulled into Vegas a couple of hours ago. After a long piss and checking into my room, I found myself here— the Gypsy Club, according to the sign outside.

The waitress notices me eyeing the girl dancing on stage. "Want me to fetch her for you after she's done?"

I shake my head. "Nah, I'm on the clock. Maybe next time."

She then squints her eyes, giving me the once-over. "On the clock? What are you, a cop?"

I shake my head.

"A private dick?"

"Yeah, something like that," I answer, trying to placate her. I just want her to get me my drink.

Satisfied with my made-up answer, she finally leaves. What if I had been a cop? Would I have been treated differently? She probably just wanted to know if I needed greasing under the table—or something else under the table to keep me from looking around the joint too closely.

I wasn't lying much. Private dick, journalist—no difference. We all walk in the same shit. The shit I'm covering is the Beatles. The paper sent me from LA to snap some pictures and write up their Vegas concert before the little punks hit the Hollywood Bowl. They want to get ahead of it—capitalize on the excitement.

Beatlemania, they call it. I don't get it—the moppy hair, the screaming girls. I'm a Sinatra guy, but I couldn't pass up an all-expense-paid trip to Vegas.

My eyes return to the tiny go-go dancer on stage. God, she's got some perky little double-A batteries. I'm fifty-two years old and can't get my cock up for shit, but that doesn't stop me from thinking about it. I should feel ashamed of myself, embarrassed. But I don't. That's the trouble.

"Hi there, stranger," a big dolled-up blond says, sitting down at my table, blocking my view. "Care for some company?"

Noticing my visible annoyance, the blond glances at the stage and tosses her hair back. "Trust me, you aren't missing much. Wouldn't you rather have something you can smother your face into?" she asks, leaning forward, revealing an amazing set of breasts.

I won't lie—they are a gift from God. Something Jayne Mansfield would've been envious of.

I lean back in my chair and light a cigarette. "Forget it, I ain't shoppin' tonight," I say, blowing a ring of smoke into her face.

She doesn't flinch. Hmm. Maybe I should keep this one around for a while. I offer her a cigarette.

"Is it because you're on the job?" she asks, plucking one from my case with manicured fingernails. "That's what Carol said—that you were a private...dick." She emphasizes the last word, lighting her cigarette with a table candle, her smoky eyes never leaving mine.

I play along. "Yeah, got a big case I'm working. Very wealthy client."

After blowing a cloud of smoke out the side of her mouth, she offers her hand.

"I'm Nancy."

"Frank," I reply, shaking it. My name isn't Frank, and hers probably isn't Nancy.

"So, Nancy, where are you from?" I ask, trying to keep my eyes off her bosom, though she doesn't seem to mind me staring.

"Las Vegas," she replies, taking another drag off her cigarette. "Born and raised."

"Born and raised? Don't see that too often."

"Yup. Fourth generation," she says, a hint of pride in her voice. "My great-grandparents were sent by Brigham Young to colonize the valley."

Funny, isn't it? Las Vegas, founded by do-gooding Mormons. This girl, though, with her tits hanging out—she certainly doesn't exude any "do-goodness."

Suddenly, the cocktail waitress reappears with a couple of drinks. She hands me mine and sets the other one down in front of the blond, calling her by name. I guess her name really is Nancy. I'll stick with Frank, though.

"Thanks, Carol," Nancy says, flashing the waitress a smile. Then she turns back to me. "I hope you don't mind. I asked her to put my drink on your tab."

I should have known better. Little Miss Mormon just wanted a free drink outta me. What the hell, I'm enjoying the scenery. I smile and raise my glass. "Cheers." God, that's smooth.

Suddenly, Nancy's eyes widen as she glances over my shoulder. Without warning, she ducks under the table, hiding beneath the white tablecloth. She crawls over to me, placing her hands on my knees and spreading my thighs.

"Whoa, what are you doing down there?" I ask, though I ain't complaining. Her hands feel good on my knees.

"Shhh," she whispers, her head now between my legs. "Don't look, but there's a man who just walked in. He wants to kill me."

I casually glance toward the entrance. There's an older man, gangly and balding, dressed kinda square in a dark suit and tie. He's got a couple of goons with him—bigger, younger guys with perfectly coiffed blond hair.

"What, the older guy with a couple of Ken dolls?" I ask, chuckling a bit.

Then a sharp pain wells up in my groin, the kind that starts in your stomach and climbs up your throat. The little hussy just flicked me in the balls with her middle finger.

"It isn't funny," she whispers harshly. "I gotta get out of here."

Her head's now poking up between my legs, scanning the room. "Did you drive or take a cab?" she asks, looking up at me.

I put my hands on her head, gently pushing her back down. "My car's parked out back. Why do they want to kill you?" I ask, deciding to play along with her paranoia, wondering what drug she's coming down from.

"I can't tell you right now, just that I have to leave," she says, motioning for her drink. After I hand it to her, she downs it like a lush and gives me the empty glass. "Can you drive me home?" she asks, almost begging, her eyes pouting up at me from under the table. She looks desperate, like every addict does when they're jonesing for their next hit.

I take a deep breath and glance at my watch. It's still early. I'd planned on hitting the craps table later and passing out in bed by 2:00 a.m.—plenty of time to sober up before hobbling over to the convention center with my camera in the morning. If I left now, I could drop her off and still stick to the plan.

Why the fuck not? I give Nancy a quick nod, and she smiles. Her hand then gently brushes my cock, lingering before retracting. Thanking me…or maybe apologizing for the earlier flick in the nuts. She's a pro, knowing just the right amount of pressure to make it all feel better.

"What kind of car do you drive?" she asks.

"Chevy Malibu coupe," I answer. "Brand new, gold. Can't miss it."

It's a beautiful car. I picked it up earlier in the year to replace my '53 Lincoln. It's what the kids were driving. What can I say? After the wife left me ten years ago, I was in the middle of a mid-life crisis.

"Okay," she continues. "When you stand up to leave, I'll crawl out from behind you and head out the back door. I'll meet you in your car. Is it locked?"

I nod and pass her the keys under the table.

After a count of three, I stand up as tall as I can, making room for her to scurry out. When I see her disappear behind the rear curtain, I head up front to settle the tab. As I'm paying the bartender, I suddenly have one of those what-the-fuck-are-you-thinking moments and bolt outside without even collecting my change, fully expecting my brand-new car to be gone.

"Thank God," I say out loud, letting out a deep breath when I see it's still there. I check the doors—they're unlocked—and climb inside. Where the fuck is she? I should've kept the keys so I could just leave, I chide myself.

"Hey there," she says, surprising me as her arms wrap around my neck from behind. She'd been hiding in the back seat. "Shit, you almost gave me a heart attack."

She then flashes my press credentials.

"Kelly O'Connor, *Los Angeles Times*. I thought you said your name was Frank and you were a private detective," she says, eyeing me suspiciously. "What's up with a girly first name?"

I never liked my first name. Named after my grandfather, Cillian Fitzpatrick. But no one ever knew how to pronounce Cillian, so they just called me Kelly. I gave out just as many bloody noses as I got in the schoolyard because of that name. But I learned to hold my own.

"Hey, those were in the glove box. What else did you grab outta there?"

"You mean this?" she asks, waving my service revolver in the other hand.

"Jesus Christ, put that thing down. It ain't exactly registered," I say, looking around the parking lot, hoping no one saw it.

I never returned my revolver after the war like I was supposed to. I hid it in my sea bag. Hell, with so many of us coming home at once, no one even bothered to check.

We saw some crazy shit in the Pacific. Half my unit never made it back. "Oorah" to those young Marine bastards—may you rot in hell. I still dream about those guys—sometimes I see them standing right next to me, telling me I was the lucky one. I don't have the heart to tell them I was just hiding in the bush with a piece of shrapnel in my ass, too scared to give away my position.

One good thing came out of the service, though. After getting wounded in Guadalcanal, the Corps gave me a camera and taught me how to use it. I mean, how to use it in the middle of a firefight kinda way. I captured images of the real Marine— the kind with mud on his face and a middle finger raised. Raw and unfiltered. It's what got me the job with the paper when I got back.

I immediately check the gun when she hands it back to me. It's still loaded. After returning it to the glove box, I pat the front seat, motioning for her to get up front. "I ain't no taxi driver," I say.

She hangs my press credentials around her neck, squeezes between the bucket seats, and plops down next to me.

"Nice car," she says, glancing around before grabbing a duffel bag from the back seat. She places it in her lap and opens it—inside is her whole closet: a few outfits, makeup, and a wig. She pulls out a small leather purse from beneath the mess, opens it, and stuffs it with a wad of cash she had hidden down her bra.

Pretending not to look, I light a cigarette with the car lighter and offer her one. She takes it, but instead of using the lighter, she pulls mine outta my mouth and lights hers with it. The girl's really working me, wanting more than just a lift home.

Putting the car in gear, I slowly drive around the back of the building to where the parking lot meets the street. Suddenly, she ducks down low in her seat. One of the blondies from the club is out front, scoping the lot. I act like nothing's up and pull out onto the street—not too fast, don't want to draw his attention.

"Shit," she says, now sitting up and looking behind us. "Do you think he saw me?"

I glance at the rearview mirror. "I don't think so," I say, but I keep checking back just in case.

"So where exactly is…home?" I ask. I'd like to get her out of my hair so I can get to the craps table and then to my comfy bed at the Desert Inn.

She doesn't respond, just stares out the window like a scared little girl. The whole thing must've really spooked her. I want to ask who the hell those guys were, but I can tell she's not in the mood to talk.

"Do you think we can just drive around for a bit? Or maybe go somewhere? It's still early," she finally says.

As much as I want to be rid of her, I feel kinda bad. Oh, what the hell, I could use the company. "Wanna play some craps?" I ask.

She turns to me, eyes wide. "Only if you let me blow your dice," she says, raising an eyebrow and grinning. If the girl is one thing, she is a fucking tease.

An hour after arriving at the hotel, we're sitting at the bar—broke, except for the hundred bucks in reserve chips I always keep stuffed down my pants. I'd been up a couple grand, but then I made the mistake of listening to her. I can still hear her voice purring in my ear.

"Trust me," she says, placing all my chips on the "COME" line. "I can make anything come," she brags, blowing on my dice, her lips mimicking a blowjob around an imaginary shaft. I should've trusted my gut, not my johnson. I'd been rolling sevens all night, but I was bound to run out eventually.

Which is why we're sitting here now.

I'm ready to cut my losses and get back out there with my reserve chips. After this last drink, I tell myself, then I'll ditch her. But then I notice my media credentials still hanging around her neck. Shit, I forgot she had them. I motion for her to hand them over.

"Are you still gonna take me home?" she asks, holding the credentials just out of my reach. She smells me boltin' for the door.

"They got cabs out front," I say, slipping a five-dollar bill on the bar.

She quickly shoves the fiver into her purse.

"Well, before I return this to you...Kelly O'Connor," she pouts, glancing down at my name badge, "will you at least tell me what this is for?"

"The Beatles," I reply. "There's a press junket before the concert tomorrow night."

Her eyes light up like a Christmas tree. "You're going to the Beatles concert?"

I shrug, playing it cool.

Noticing my lack of enthusiasm, she squints at me. "You don't seem very excited. You know, tickets were impossible to get. It's supposed to be wild."

"Call me a square, but I'm a Sinatra kinda guy. I don't like wild." My hand stays outstretched.

She slaps it down with a giggle, then takes the pass and holds it close to her chest. "Well then, let me go in your place. I could certainly pass for a Kelly," she says, tracing my name on the credentials with her forefinger. "What I would do for a ticket," I hear her mumble to herself.

I shake my head. It's been a long day, and I need a pick-me-up. Sick of her games, I reach into my coat pocket, grab an upper, and down it with the last of my drink.

Ahh, that's better.

"What's that?" she asks, noticing the pill. She reaches out her hand. "You mustn't be stingy now."

I let out a deep sigh. "If I give you one, will you take a cab and go home?"

She nods eagerly, her eyes as large as saucers.

I retrieve one, stand up, and reluctantly place it in her expectant hand. "Nice meeting you, Nancy," I say, straightening my coat and hoping to never see her again.

Famous last words, right? I should've just gone straight to my hotel room when I realized I'd forgotten them. I was in the bathroom, retrieving the stash of chips from down my pants, when it hit me—I'd walked away without my credentials. Fuck. I need those for the concert.

Rushing back to the bar, I pause about fifty feet away when I see what's going on. Nancy's arguing with the two blondie boys. They must've seen us leave the club and followed us. I hesitate, wondering if I really need the credentials. Maybe I could just flash my driver's license at the event tomorrow and leave this mess behind.

But now they're really roughing her up.

I know I shouldn't get involved.

But I really need those press credentials.

Taking a deep breath, I approach the scuffle. "Gentlemen, what seems to be the problem?"

Nancy suddenly breaks free and rushes over, hiding behind me with her head peeking over my shoulder. "You came back for me," she says, breathless and surprised.

"The only problem here is yours, bud," one of the Ken dolls replies, hiking up his shirt to show a gun stuffed down the front of his pants.

I raise my hands to chest level and turn slowly, pointing to the lanyard around Nancy's neck. "I just came back for my credentials. Then I'll be on my way."

Nancy's eyes flash with anger, and she gives me a hard shove. I stumble, caught off guard by her aggression. She throws my credentials on the floor. "You're all bastards," she yells. "Every one of you."

Before I can retrieve them, the other goon motions me back and picks them up, reading them. After pocketing my badge, he gestures to his partner, who's already circled around and pinned Nancy's arms, his gun discreetly pressed into her back. The guy in front then motions for both of us to follow him.

Why the fuck didn't I just go up to my room?

After a tense elevator ride up to the seventh floor, we're led to a room at the end of the hall. The older guy from the club answers the door—the boss. There's something off about this crew. I've been around enough wise guys to recognize their mannerisms, the cadence in their speech. These guys aren't Mafia, but they're dangerous all the same. I decide to keep my mouth shut.

"I said just the girl," the boss says, eyeing me up and down. "Why'd you bring him?"

The guy behind me reaches into his pocket and hands the boss my credentials.

"He saw everything. Figured you'd want him taken care of."

Reading my badge out loud, the boss lets out a deep breath and approaches his man. "Where's your sense of compassion, Hyrum?" he says, wetting his finger and fixing the blondie's tussled hair. "We must demonstrate to Mr. O'Connor that we are a charitable people—a righteous people." He turns then, locking his steely gray eyes on mine, and something in that gaze twists inside me. It's like a switch being flipped.

Suddenly, it's there—the trigger. The fucking jungle comes rushing in, uninvited. My unit calling out to me. Kill the bastards, they say. Shoot the fucking Jap bastards. I fight to keep control, to push it all down. It's just a dream, I tell myself. It's all a fucking dream. Then, just as quickly, it fades, and I'm back in the room, refocusing on the boss's eyes.

"And we must thank our guest for returning our long-lost daughter," he continues, motioning toward Nancy.

"Your daughter?" she screams. "I'm not going back!" But a strong hand quickly silences her.

The boss reaches into his coat pocket and pulls out a stack of hundred-dollar bills, counting out ten. He hands them to me along with my badge, continuing, "For saving our dear sister from the clutches of evil."

There's something really creepy about the way he talks— the pacing, the creaky voice—it's almost biblical. Then I remember Nancy mentioning her Mormon background. Holy fuck, she's part of some Mormon sect. I glance over at Nancy, but there's nothing I can do. I feel sorry for her, but I still take the money.

Suddenly, one of the blondies yelps as Nancy bites his hand and breaks free. The boss calmly motions for him to stand down.

"I was fourteen when I married you. Fourteen," she screams, her voice cracking with anger. She then turns to me. "I ran away two years ago. Thought he'd give up the chase by now." She retrieves her purse from the floor, where it landed during the scuffle.

"Nancy, dear, I'll never give you up," he says, his tone disturbingly calm. "We've been sealed together for time and all eternity."

"For time and all eternity? We'll see about that," she snaps, pulling my gun from her purse. Shit, how did she get ahold of it again? She must've snatched it out of the glove box while I was distracted with the valet.

She aims it at him, and the blondie boys immediately draw their pistols.

"Everybody just relax," I say, adrenaline pumping through my veins, eyes darting between them. Stay calm, I tell myself. Keep it together. But I can feel it—the jungle beating down the door.

"I'm not going back," she screams.

She starts to turn the gun on herself. That gun turns real easy in the hand—like it's made for this. I've been there a hundred times, but always chickened out at the last second. But I see it in her eyes—she won't.

Panic rises, the screams of my unit echo in the distance after a mortar shell hits. I may be injured, but I'm done hiding in this fucking elephant grass.

Instinct takes over. Without thinking, I leap forward and knock the gun from her hands.

The gun hits the ground, two shots ring out, and the jungle fully closes in. I drop down, grab the gun, and squeeze off three quick rounds. The Japs are ambushing us, but I'm faster, hitting them square in the head. They're dead. My men are safe.

But then I look down—blood pooling from my leg. They got me. Bleeding out fast. Those bastards hit an artery.

The shots fade, and I blink—back to this shitty room. The Mormon boss and his goons—dead on the floor. A pair of eyes suddenly look down at me, warm and pure. "I didn't just save my own ass this time," I say to the eyes.

I don't feel any pain. Only peace—finally.

But the eyes turn cold and detached before leaving me, and I feel someone rifling through my clothes. I realize she ain't no angel. It's Nancy. She takes my keys, my remaining chips, the reward money, even my press credentials. Now she's going through my jacket. The pills—she takes every last goddamned one.

Should I warn her, the little tramp?

Nah. I just lie there and chuckle as I'm bleeding out. I'll see you real soon, Nancy darling. Don't forget the credentials.

Why the fuck didn't I just go up to my room?

Kurt Larsen, a retired casino gaming exec, kicks off his "third act" as a novelist. A pro animator and music composer, he spins suspenseful stories shaped by years of art and sound. With his wife, he launched *beCurious*, a kids' YouTube channel mixing fun and purpose. Married with two kids, he lives in Reno, NV, raising his family while finishing his debut novel, *The Lost Paintings of Pieter van Dijk*. His work blends an artist's eye with a gambler's knack for keeping you hooked.

Fools Fall in Love

By Lisa Ard

THE ALBUM DROPPED on the turntable, and my heart followed. I wiped tears from my face and placed the needle on a groove. Notes of a strumming guitar emerged, along with Elvis's first words: "Love Me Tender." My brief life was over. Tomorrow Elvis Presley would marry Priscilla Beaulieu in Palm Springs.

Since their engagement on Christmas Day 1966, I'd searched news reports to learn about the nuptials. While walking home from school, I prayed that the light bulbs flashing above my head on the Las Vegas Strip would spark an idea to stop the wedding. If I could reach Palm Springs, I'd find a way.

But Dad wasn't up for a trip to Southern California. "Las Vegas is desert," he'd said. "Why would we drive to Palm Springs?"

I didn't have an answer, but he didn't need one. He wasn't blind. Magazines and newspapers with articles about Elvis littered our hotel suite.

Last week, my favorite maid picked up my March issue of *Elvis Monthly* magazine.

"He's a dreamy one, Rachel," Susan said. "Looks like he'll get away from us, though."

She never had a chance. Susan was at least thirty. I, however, was thirteen, nearly the age Priscilla was when she met Elvis in Germany. Now, Priscilla is twenty-one. I figured I had the advantage of youth. For months, I'd schemed on how

I might meet Elvis and steal him away from the pretty brunette. He visited Vegas often, either to relax or perform.

Elvis crooned the line about how I made his life complete.

I kissed the album cover and took in his heavily lidded gaze, dark pompadour, and sultry expression.

Dad cleared his throat. I hadn't heard him come in. I whirled about and dropped the picture of the man I'd loved ever since *Viva Las Vegas* opened in theaters four years ago.

"Honey." Dad looked at the floor, avoiding my tear-stained face. Not sure who was more embarrassed. "I need you to stay in your room while I hold a meeting."

Being a single dad of a teenage girl was impossibly hard, according to Dad's late-night whisperings on the phone with his sister. Aunt Jane tried to convince Dad to move back to Oregon.

"Do you want Rachel to grow up in Sin City?"

Dad gave the same answer every time. "I'm doing the best I can, Jane. Besides, my job's too good to leave."

Milton Prell hired Dad as entertainment director for the Aladdin Hotel before the property reopened with an Oriental theme last year. It screamed luxury. The stories of the Arabian Nights splashed across the walls in huge, colorful murals. Modern slot machines. Bars with flying carpets. I loved the glowing gold lights of the fifteen-foot genie's lamp. Plus, riding the escalators was fun.

Each morning before I left for school, Dad knotted his skinny black tie, shrugged on a fitted suit jacket, and hit the casino floor. Everyone knew him. Showgirls, blackjack dealers, servers, and performers. Inside our suite, he was my dad. Outside, he was Mr. Rollo.

Dad never held meetings in our suite.

"But it's Sunday," I said. "I want to go to the pool."

"Stay put," he pleaded. "For maybe an hour."

I waited until I heard his footsteps padding away, then I cracked open my door.

Our suite's doorbell sang an *Arabian Nights* tune. Dad swung open the double-doors and welcomed the mysterious guest.

"Tom, come in!" Dad said. "Drink?"

I peeked through a crack to see a man smoking a stogie and wearing a cowboy hat with a rolled brim. I'd recognize his oversized ears, jowls, and rounded belly anywhere. This was Colonel Tom Parker, Elvis's manager.

Dad poured two bourbons, neat. They took a seat on our matching chenille sofas and got down to business.

"This is a surprise," Dad said. "What happened to Palm Springs?"

Parker chomped on his cigar. "Damned paparazzi won't let them out of the house."

I'd studied pictures of "The House of Tomorrow," the Palm Springs home Elvis rented. I imagined lounging on its circular sofa, snuggling up with Elvis, and taking in the dreamy view of palm trees and mountains through the floor-to-ceiling windows. Priscilla was noticeably absent from my daydream.

"Elvis called Frank. It's all arranged," Parker said. "The wedding party will sneak out the back, where a limo will take them to Sinatra's jet. They'll land in Vegas at 3:00 a.m. and go straight to the courthouse for the marriage license," Parker said in clipped tones. "I need security here and an escort to Milton's suite."

The rest of the conversation was a blur. Sixty guests arriving. Not to leave the room once notified of the wedding. Plans for a six-tiered cake. Names piped on at the last minute.

"I'll take care of it," Dad said. The two men clinked glasses, and shortly after, Colonel Tom left.

I had a chance.

I slid "Love Me Tender" in its sleeve and shelved it with the rest of my Elvis collection. My other albums—birthday gifts from friends—sat mostly unplayed. The Beatles and the Byrds had nothing on Elvis.

Aretha Franklin's "I Never Loved a Man the Way I Love You" caught my eye. It was a sign. Tomorrow I would say those very words to Elvis. He'd fall madly in love with me, and I'd take Priscilla's place.

I threaded the album on the spindle, let it drop, and plunked down the needle. I belted out those great questions and answers, while I came up with a plan.

Step one: In the next twelve hours, become irresistible.

Step two: Storm into the suite, declare my undying love for Elvis, and catch him when he falls for me.

It wouldn't be easy, but I lived in the city of impossible dreams and extraordinary magic.

I looked myself over in the mirror hanging on my closet door. I had pretty blue eyes, at least that's what Dad said. My skin had a few pimples. Nothing a little Max Factor Erace couldn't conceal. My hair was not as long or luxurious as Priscilla's; this needed sorting. At five feet five inches tall, I'd have to wear heels. Elvis was six feet tall—six feet two inches with the pompadour. Finally, my clothes: preppy Mary Janes, colorful knee-high socks, a plaid skirt, and a boring cardigan. I dressed like a child.

I knew just where to go.

Backstage was off-limits to me under normal circumstances. But being the boss's daughter came with privileges. I knew every secret passage on the property. Plus, employees favored me to get in good with Mr. Rollo. Basically, I had the run of the place.

Three shows ran nightly at the Baghdad Theatre, including the topless Pussy Cats Galore Revue. The girls were surprisingly talented musicians. I didn't plan to reveal my flat chest, but they knew how to attract a man, and I needed all the help I could get, quickly.

"Does your daddy know you're here?" Linda perched on a stool before an illuminated mirror as she rimmed her eyes with liquid black liner.

I ignored her question, sank to the floor, and leaned against her dressing counter.

"Heavens! What's the matter?" She stared down at me with one eye sporting two-inch fake eyelashes.

The other girl band members busied themselves fixing their makeup, powdering their bare chests with glitter, or applying pasties to their nipples. They towered over me with their white leather boots, long tan legs, and sequined bikini bottoms. Trumpets, French horns, and tubas glistened between the girls and the mirrors. I was certain of one thing: The men in the audience didn't come for the music.

"I need a makeover," I whispered.

"Oh la la," Linda cried. "Is it a boy?"

I nodded.

"Deborah! Barbara! Girls! Get over here."

An hour later, I'd been painted and primped. Although Linda promised she'd used a light touch, I didn't recognize my face under its beige coating. Berry-colored lipstick plumped my mouth. Black eyeliner and sky-blue shadow created the doe eyes that were all the fashion. Julie offered a stand with one of her wigs, a darker, longer version of my hair. I'd sleep on my back tonight to preserve my dolled-up look and slip the wig on in the morning.

"Do you have anything to wear?" Linda asked. "I'm afraid we're short in the wardrobe department. We've got boots, but little else."

That was an understatement.

Unfortunately, my closet was an advertisement for the Sears catalog. That gave me one option: the clothes Mom left behind.

After two hours with my very own Avon lady, I zigzagged between the dinging slot machines, past the blackjack dealers throwing out cards and the short-skirted waitresses selling cigarettes. I avoided the service elevator and the employees who might mention my makeover to Dad. When I reached our floor, I peeked out of the elevator crammed with tourists to make sure the coast was clear, then dashed down the hall to our suite.

"Hello?" I called out. Silence greeted me.

I sneaked into Dad's room and searched the back of his closet.

He'd kept three of Mom's dresses after she died. First, her wedding gown. Right for the day, but too presumptuous. Second, a maternity frock, the one she'd worn when he drove her to the hospital to deliver me. Out of the question. A dark blue cocktail dress. It would do.

The silk glistened against his black wool suits. I stroked the fabric and tried to remember the feel of her touch, the scent of her shampoo, or the sound of her voice. My heart sank two inches in my chest. I could use a mother right now.

Grabbing the hanger, I dashed back to my room. I shrugged off my Mayberry clothes and slipped on the halter-style dress with its pleated skirt. Mom had won Dad over while dancing in this.

Maybe she was with me after all.

I twirled in front of the mirror. With a little imagination, I could be Ginger on *Gilligan's Island*. I just needed gorgeous red hair and a chest. I adjusted the wig and practiced my opening words.

"Why, Elvis! What brings you here?"

That reminds him he's marrying Priscilla.

"Elvis, I've waited all my life for you." Well, I had hours to work on it.

***

My alarm trilled at 7:00 a.m. on May 1, 1967, the most important day of my life. Dad was long gone, tending to the "special" guests.

I jumped up and collected my gear from the closet. My eyes were crusty and red from sleeping with eyeliner on. Linda had sent me off with fake eyelashes, and I wrestled with putting them on straight. I reapplied the borrowed lipstick. With the wig attached, my teased-up tresses hung down the middle of

128

my back. I padded my bra with tissues for my very own foam domes. I zipped up the white leather boots. Getting myself together took some time, but the result was unbelievable. I danced to Elvis's "That's All Right" to rally for the big day.

The guests would have arrived at 5:30 a.m., according to the Colonel. It was almost nine. Milton Prell had invited Elvis and Priscilla to his suite for a morning wedding, although I didn't know the exact time. I walked unsteadily but carefully in my high-heeled boots.

The climb in the service elevator took forever. Sweat beaded along my hairline and under the wig. How did women wear these without melting? I pulled a tissue from each boob—to keep them even—and dabbed my face. The bell dinged for the top floor, and the doors opened into the flower- and candle-filled suite.

"I now pronounce you man and wife. You may kiss the bride."

My breath caught in my throat. Elvis leaned in and cupped his hand around his bride's face. His lips met hers instead of mine. My eyes blurred, and I choked out a faint cry.

I might have escaped eternal mortification had I not stumbled forward when the elevator doors closed on me and bumped into a middle-aged woman dressed to the nines. The cheers of the guests drowned out her bawl. But our staggering dance caught the attention of the one man I'd hoped to avoid.

Dad made a beeline across the space for me.

With tears building, I apologized to the lady scowling at me and escaped. No time to wait for the elevator. I slipped into the powder room off the entry.

The lavender wallpaper, plush carpet, and light purple sinks and countertops invited one to linger. I'd rather stay in this bathroom, the size of our living room, than argue with Dad. I limped over and twisted the gold-plated faucet, then leaned down to gulp cold water and splash my cheeks.

Snatching a towelette from a stack on the counter, I dried my face. Black, beige, and pink streaked across the crisp white fabric. What had I been thinking? I stared at my hopeless self in the mirror, with tissue leaking out under my armpit, a slightly askew wig, patchy eyeliner, and blotchy skin. I'd never stood a chance.

The squeaking door sent me scurrying into the toilet stall. I locked myself inside and sat down on the porcelain throne. Maybe I could wait for everyone to leave?

I heard a clatter on the counter. I peeked out to see Priscilla applying a fresh coat of lipstick.

She spotted me in the mirror and smiled. "Well, hello." She turned toward me. "He kissed my lipstick right off."

What could I say? Didn't one wish the bride the best? But she had everything already. Her white empire-waist dress billowed. The rhinestone tiara and veil framed her dark hair and bright eyes. But it was the grape-sized diamond ring on her finger that caught my eye.

Priscilla followed my gaze and held out her hand. "I can hardly believe it myself."

I emerged from the closet and joined her at the mirror. I wanted to claw her to pieces, rip the gorgeous dress from her body, scream that she'd stolen the only man in the world for me.

And then Priscilla handed me the shiny gold tube. "Do you want some?"

Was she being kind because she'd noticed my tears or because I'd been hiding in the toilet stall? I smeared the pearly pink lipstick on my mouth. She passed me tissues and pointed at my collapsing dress front. I padded my chest while she straightened my wig and tucked in a few loose tendrils. She wiped the remnants of my eyeliner away.

Priscilla peered over my shoulder and caught my eye in the mirror. "Everyone needs a little help sometimes."

I returned the lipstick, and our hands touched. Not just the diamond dazzled.

"It looks beautiful on you," I said.

Priscilla smiled, then dropped the gold tube in her clutch. She looked one last time in the mirror and smacked her lips together. "Duty calls. Off to a press conference." Before leaving, Mrs. Elvis Presley turned and said, "Your day will come."

I watched her go, and hope filled me. I stood a little taller. Glancing in the mirror, I pulled the wig off and finger-combed my light brown hair, twisting the strands into waves. The lipstick stayed, but the blue eyeshadow came off. I plumped up my foam domes. After all, everyone needs a little help sometimes.

When the noise died down, I left my refuge. In the enormous suite, cleaners extinguished candles, gathered flowers, and vacuumed away the footprints of the witnesses to the wedding of the year.

Within minutes, I'd returned to our empty living quarters. The rooms looked the same. Only I had changed. I kicked off the go-go boots and placed them by my door. My mother's cocktail dress found a spot in my closet. Someday I'd wear it again. For now, I shrugged on a pair of Capri pants and tossed on a T-shirt.

I hit the turntable's switch and dropped on my newest album. The music lifted me up, and my feet moved to the beat.

The words about love being true in fairy tales and not meant for me...The Monkees knew my heart.

I twirled and hopped, swinging my arms in circles, dancing away my blues, until I was out of breath. I sang along. I was in love. I was a believer!

When the song stopped, I flipped over the album cover. Davy Jones gazed back. What a foxy guy.

Lisa Ard is the author of the historical fiction novel *Brighter Than Her Fears*, which is based on her great-great-grandmother's experience in 19th-century western North Carolina. Her previously published children's books include *Fright Flight, Dream Team* and the Kay Snow award finalist *Saving Halloween*. When not writing, Lisa enjoys reading, hiking, golfing, and sharing her love of history as a bike tour docent with the Palm Springs Historical Society. She and her husband live (and golf) in both Palm Springs and Portland, Oregon. Lisa's website is www.authorlisaard.com.

Twenty Minutes Until Showtime

Linda Saether

"TWENTY MINUTES, Mr. Presley."

Elvis acknowledged the stage manager with a silent nod, one that Joe Esposito translated into a dismissive wave as he stepped out into the hall. Years together had taught him and the other members of the Memphis Mafia to read their boss with the precision of long-married couples, though none of them would admit they were watching him more closely these days. They orbited him like planets around a dimming sun, their gravitational dance growing more precarious with each passing show. The Vegas Hilton had become their universe, its golden elevators and mirrored hallways a maze they'd purposefully memorized through countless nights of shows, parties, and increasingly frequent medical emergencies.

Alone in his dressing room, Elvis reached for the familiar orange bottle, letting a few blue pills tumble into his palm. Diazepam—that's what Dr. Nick called them, though Elvis had long stopped keeping track of names. He swallowed them with lukewarm Pepsi, grimacing at his reflection. Dr. Nick's voice echoed in his head—some to calm the nerves, others to help him sleep, and more to wake him up again. The cycle had become more choreographed than his stage moves, though he couldn't quite remember when the pills had become as essential as breathing. The doctor's promises of "just enough to get you through the show" had evolved into a symphony of prescriptions that played through every hour of his day.

The dressing room walls were covered with photos— snapshots of a life lived at full throttle. There he was with Johnny Cash at Sun Records, when they were both young and hungry. Another showed him with Priscilla and their daughter at Graceland before the divorce had carved another hollow space in his heart. Lisa Marie was eight now, growing up in a world that knew her daddy only as an idol carved in rhinestones and gold, and who she knew for sure hung the moon.

He picked up his old Martin D-18, different from the gleaming showpieces he used on stage. He had bought it back in '56, when he was still stunned by the success of "Heartbreak Hotel." His fingers found the frets without thought, muscle memory carrying him back to Sunday mornings in Memphis. The first chord rang out clear and true, a fragment of "Amazing Grace" that his Mama used to sing. Back then, music had been a prayer, pure and simple, before Colonel Parker had turned it into an empire, but he still found his way back to its gospel.

The Colonel, Tom Parker, the former carnival barker who'd transformed a truck driver into a king. Elvis could still remember signing that first contract, his Mama's worried eyes watching as he traded away fifty percent of everything he would ever earn. But the Colonel had delivered on his promises, hadn't he?

From Sun Records sensation to Hollywood's golden boy, from laughingstock Vegas newcomer back in '56 to the Strip's reigning king, he'd blazed a path from Mississippi poverty to international stardom that defied imagination, his voice now as recognized in Berlin as it was in Birmingham, but in the process he had learned that even blessings had their cost.

"Colonel wants to see you, E," Red West's voice carried through the door, heavy with decades of friendship and unspoken worry. Red had been there since high school, back when they'd bonded over their shared love of gospel music and football at Humes High.

"Tell him I'm praying," Elvis replied, and it wasn't entirely a lie. These moments alone with his old guitar were the closest thing to church he had left. His fingers found the opening notes of "Peace in the Valley," and for a moment, he was back in Memphis, watching his Mama smile as he sang her favorite hymn.

"Fifteen minutes!"

Elvis turned and took in the man in the mirror. His white jumpsuit caught the light like armor, each rhinestone a tiny star in his personal constellation. It was perfect. Bill Belew had outdone himself with this one. The Phoenix suit, they called it, with its high collar and elaborate beading that traced patterns of fire down the legs. His hair was still midnight black, his face fuller than in those wild early days, but his eyes remained unchanged, blue as a Tennessee sky, with that familiar Memphis fire burning behind them. Sometimes, he wondered if that smoldering was consuming him from the inside out. Pricilla had seen it, calling him "fire-eyes" when he raged.

He thought about his first Vegas run in '56, when the New Frontier had billed him below Freddie Martin and his orchestra, with Shecky Greene as the headliner. The critics had dismissed him as a guitar-wielding juvenile delinquent, all sneer and swivel hips. "A jug of corn liquor in a bottle of champagne," one had written. Now he owned the Strip, commanding the highest-paid residency in Vegas history—one million dollars a year to play two shows a night in the Vegas Hilton's cavernous showroom, two months a year. The journey from Tupelo to this gilded cage was a story even he sometimes struggled to believe.

"You okay, Buntin?" Linda Thompson's voice carried that sweet Tennessee lilt that always brought him home as she slipped through the doorway. She'd been his anchor these past years since Priscilla left, loving the man rather than the idol. At twenty-seven, she was young enough to still be impressed by the glamour of his life, but wise enough to see through it. His eyes caught the flash of blue diamond on her finger, a random

Tuesday gift he'd given her at Graceland, transforming an ordinary moment into memory with the casual extravagance that had become his language of love.

"Ten minutes, Mr. Presley!"

The call echoed down the hallway, but Elvis kept his gaze fixed on Linda.

"I'm fine, honey," he lied, and they both let it slide. The truth was a luxury he couldn't afford, not with two thousand people waiting and the Colonel's contracts to fulfill. Linda's hand lingered on his shoulder, her touch saying what words couldn't, that she saw the tremors in his hands, noticed how the jumpsuit had to be taken out again, watched him chase pills with Pepsi and prayers. That more than anything, she wished she could help.

"Five minutes!"

This time the call had urgency in it, making Elvis straighten his shoulders beneath the weight of the Phoenix suit.

Elvis popped another pill, chasing it with more soda instead of the water Dr. Nick had recommended. The Memphis Mafia formed around him as he stepped into the hallway, childhood friends and distant cousins who'd followed him from Mississippi mud to a neon world that some believed was paradise.

The excitement of the crowd grew louder as they approached the stage. Twenty years of adoring fans still made his heart race like the first time he was at Sun Studios when he'd paid four dollars to record "My Happiness" for his Mama. Maybe that's what kept him going—not the pills or the doctors or the endless contracts, but that electric current of pure love arcing between him and the audience. In those moments, he wasn't the lonely boy from Tupelo or the troubled man in the gilded cage—he was Elvis Presley, and he could make his fans feel that the heavens could touch the earth.

"Two minutes!"

Through the halls, the opening notes of "Also Sprach Zarathustra" began to build. Elvis closed his eyes, letting the memories wash over him: his mother's voice singing hymns in their shotgun house, Sam Phillips at Sun Records telling him to do it again, Ed Sullivan's camera showing him only from the waist up, Hollywood's hollow promises, and that first Vegas failure that had led to this triumph. He thought of his twin brother, Jesse, stillborn, and wondered if somewhere in heaven Mama was holding him, watching her surviving son with pride and worry in equal measure.

The orchestra hit its crescendo, and Elvis stepped into the light. Two thousand people leaped to their feet as the opening riff of "C.C. Rider" thundered through the room. For the next two hours, he wouldn't be the man with the pills and problems, he'd give his audience exactly what they came for. The rhinestones caught the spotlight like falling stars, and somewhere in the darkness beyond the stage, a new generation of fans was discovering what their parents had known all along: that when Elvis Presley sang, magic happened, and the world stopped to listen.

Dr. Linda Saether grew up in Norway with Elvis Presley's music as the soundtrack to her childhood. Since relocating to Florida, she has followed Elvis tribute artists worldwide, gathering inspiration for her forthcoming historical essay and other Elvis tributes. When not immersed in Elvis's world, Linda works on her latest crime novel or walks Florida's tree-lined parks with her "hound dogs" Anikka and Oliver. Her acclaimed works, including *The Angel of the Penny Rose* and *What We Can't Forget*, showcase her talent for breathing life into the past while revealing the human stories behind iconic cultural moments.

Acknowledgements

Historical Novel Society North America would like to extend our heartfelt thanks to everyone who helped bring this anthology to life: the volunteers on our review team, who evaluated seventy-eight submissions and narrowed them down to the finalists; our editors, Carol M. Cram, Jenny Quinlan, and Mary K. Tilghman; and the judges who determined the winner of our first short story contest!

FIONA DAVIS is the *New York Times* bestselling author of eight historical fiction novels set in iconic New York City buildings, including *The Stolen Queen, The Magnolia Palace, The Address,* and *The Lions of Fifth Avenue,* which was a *Good Morning America* book club pick. Her articles have appeared in publications like *The Wall Street Journal* and the *Oprah* magazine. She first came to New York as an actress, but fell in love with writing after getting a master's degree at Columbia Journalism School. Her books have been translated into over twenty languages and she's based in New York City.

ELIZA (E.) KNIGHT is an award-winning, USA Today and internationally bestselling traditionally and self-published author of over eighty titles. Her historical fiction titles include, *The Mayfair Bookshop, Starring Adele Astaire, Can't We Be Friends, A Day of Fire,* and the forthcoming *Confessions of a Grammar Queen.* She also writes women's fiction with an edge as Michelle Brandon. In 2013, she was named Romance Writers of America's PRO Mentor of the Year, and in 2017 she was accepted into RWA's Honor Roll for selling over 100,000 copies of her self-published title *The Highlander's Reward*. Eliza is contracted with William Morrow, Sourcebooks, and Lake Union Publishing. She is a member of the Historical Novel Society, Novelists Inc., Women's Fiction Writers Association, and Tall Poppy Writers. She is an International Tutor for Jericho Writers' Ultimate Novel Writing Course and continues to mentor and coach writers one-on-one throughout the year.

HEATHER WEBB is an award-winning, *USA Today* and international bestselling author of eleven historical novels, including her upcoming *The Hope Keeper* (2/26), and her most recent *Queens of London* and *The Next Ship Home*. She is also a teacher of twenty-five years, a freelance editor of fifteen years, and a writing coach for TheNovelry.com. Heather truly enjoys helping writers find their voice and hone their craft. To date, her books have been translated into eighteen languages worldwide. She lives in New England with her family and two mischievous cats.

About Historical Novel Society North America

Historical Novel Society North America is a nonprofit organization providing educational and literary support to writers of historical fiction via our biennial conference, virtual events, workshops, classes, and other activities. We provide ongoing education via articles, newsletters, and chapter meetings, provide opportunities for authors to meet with industry professionals, and foster an inclusive and diverse community to honor the ways in which historical fiction can illuminate lessons from the past.

The Historical Novel Society North America Conference is the largest conference for historical fiction, growing from humble origins to a state-of-the-art conference featuring over a hundred speakers, presenting on a wide range of topics, and over five hundred attendees. Learn more at www.hns-conference.com.

Proceeds from the sale of this anthology will be used to help us continue to provide an outstanding conference experience, scholarships to students and writers from underrepresented groups, and speakers from diverse backgrounds to encourage and inspire writers to keep bringing history to life through historical fiction.

Thank you for your support!